LETTERS HOME

LETTERS HOME

MARTYN BEDFORD

'Letters Home' was published in *Leeds Stories 1* and *The Book of Leeds* (Comma Press), 'My Soul to Keep' in *Spindles* (Comma Press), 'Waiting at the Pumpkin' in *The Book of Peace* (Waterstones/Penguin) and *All Saints, No Sinners* magazine (University of Manchester 2006), 'The Sayer of the Sooth' in *Beta-Life* (Comma Press), 'In Anticipation of the Queen' in *The Independent*, 'A Missing Person's Inquiry' in *M.O Crimes of Practice* (Comma Press), 'A Representative in Automotive Components' in *Fortune Hotel* (Penguin) and 'Withen' in *Protest* (Comma Press).

First published in Great Britain in 2017 by Comma Press
www.commapress.co.uk

A CIP catalogue record of this book is available from the British Library.

ISBN-13   978 1905583751

The publisher gratefully acknowledges the support of Arts Council England.

Supported using public funding by
**ARTS COUNCIL
ENGLAND**

Printed in Great Britain by Clays Ltd, St Ives plc

For Damaris, Josie and Polly.

Contents

Contents

Letters Home

Leeds, 2003

HE COMPOSES LETTERS IN his head to his wife, and to his son, although the letters remain unwritten. It would be pointless to write them and to send them when they are almost certain not to get through. And, even if they did, they would – by association – bring risk, like an infection, to the woman and child receiving them. So, the letters are born and die in his mind. In truth, fragments of letters are what he composes. A thought, a phrase, an anecdote, snippets of information about his existence here; something he has seen or experienced which would be of interest back home. Sometimes he merely describes the view from the window of his flat, high above the city. That scrap of park down there, irregularly triangular, with its pair of goalposts and the perimeter of felled tree trunks and concrete bollards, each decorated with a car tyre. Or those terraces of grimy red-brick houses, washing strung to dry between them like carnival bunting.

They hang their laundry in the streets, here.

Or that cemetery on top of the hill, its headstones silhouetted against the sky. Or the elevated intersection of motorway that pollutes his flat with light and noise and fumes, even at night. Or the football stadium, one monolithic stand angled with its steel-grey back towards his flats like the superstructure of some vast modern factory or a gigantic warship.

1

He has been to a match there, when the visiting team was from his own country. Paul, the language tutor, paid for tickets out of his own pocket, even though he is only a volunteer. He described the match in an imaginary letter to his son. If he wrote to him for real, he would pretend that his flat overlooked Old Trafford, rather than Elland Road; that he'd been to watch David Beckham, Ryan Giggs and Ruud van Nistelrooy.

Whenever Beckham took a corner, he was almost close enough for me to reach out and touch him.

He'd mentioned this to Paul, on the way to their seats ('My son and me, we are actually the Man U supporters'), and the language tutor had laughed and clapped him on the shoulder, telling him to keep his voice down if he wanted to get out of the stadium in one piece. Paul also warned him not to celebrate if the team from his country scored; then it was his turn to laugh and he had to explain that, back home, this team was his own team's enemy – its rival – and that he hated them as much as Leeds fans hated Manchester United. He tried to do this without giving the impression he was ungrateful for the ticket.

Later, in the pub, Paul taught him the song: 'You're scum and you know you are!' He already knew this word, from the slogan daubed on the door to his flat and – meaning to make a joke of this – he'd asked the tutor if his support for Man U might be the actual reason for the graffiti? But the sentence was a difficult construction and the humour seemed lost on Paul. The following evening the Englishman had turned up unannounced at the flat with paint and a brush; but he had already obliterated the message himself, so they smoked and talked and drank coffee together instead.

★

The classes are going well, but I am still having to translate everything into English in my head before I can say it aloud. This makes me seem stupid. Even quite young children here sound more intelligent than me.

Sometimes, in his letters, he describes his flat. His bed is a single mattress on the floor; the table where he eats his meals is a desk that, evidently, once belonged in a school. He has set himself the 'project' of noting down all of the inscriptions scored into its surface in the hope that Paul will make sense of those he can't decipher for himself. Some are essentially the same as you would expect to find on school desks back home, or anywhere, while others are impenetrably, idiosyncratically, English. There was a colleague in the department where he used to work who would've turned such material into a paper on the cross-cultural hieroglyphics of youth culture.

I have a microwave oven, a transistor radio...

a fridge and a two-ring cooker, and there is a shower-head attached to the taps in the bath. There is a gas heater in the bedroom and another in the living room, and a brown imitation leather sofa, fissured with age, that adheres to his skin when he sits in shorts and T-shirt to listen to the radio or to watch the portable television someone has donated. He gets out whenever he can. Tries to fill the hours, days, weeks and months of waiting. In addition to reporting periodically to the office where his application is being processed, there is food to be shopped for and the language classes to attend. Also, each day, he visits the library to read, as best he can, some of the newspapers.

I cannot find any books in our language. Though they do have a small section of German literature, so at least I'm able to read something.

He has read, or re-read, *The Trial* and *The Tin Drum* and some stories by Peter Handke because, irrespective of his politics, he is a brilliant writer. He would like to learn English well enough, one day, to read Camus again. *The Outsider* would be apt, though he is uncertain whether he would identify with the alienated white anti-hero or the young Arab he shoots dead. He discusses books, after a fashion, with Paul. He is glad of the friendship. But conscious that, if he was one of those who took to theft or pimping or drug-dealing or drunken brawling in the streets, his tutor might not be so ready to treat him to the football or to come round with a pot of paint.

★

The fragments of composition are not just about himself – he asks after her, too, and his son, despite knowing that their replies, like his questions, will remain unwritten and unread. He is afraid for them, though he tries not to betray this in his letters. He worries, apart from anything else, that his wife will no longer be able to work.

'What does she do?' Paul said, the night of the smoking and coffee-drinking.

'My wife job?'

'Does she work?'

'She is pharm-siss.'

'A pharmacist?'

'Yes, *a* pharmasiss. A phar-ma-cist.'

Paul looked again at the photograph and said his wife must be an intelligent woman. From the way he studied the picture, it was more than her intelligence that impressed him. In fairness, the Englishman was honest enough to say so.

As Paul handed the photograph back, he said: 'She's very pretty.'

'She has shop – a shop. A *drugstore*.' He grinned. 'Like Boots, only not like Boots.'

This was what he was reduced to: feeling pleased with himself for knowing the name of an English pharmacy.

He pictured her that first time, tipping pills into a triangular plastic counting tray. One cuff of her white uniform had ridden up above her wrist to reveal a pattern of fine dark hairs. He recalled her absorbed concentration as she transferred the tablets from the frame into a small bottle. Then her smile,

4

as she handed it to him. They told people they had met thanks to an acute ear infection ('He asked when was my lunch break, and I told him one-thirty, and he said: "Pardon?"').

Paul looked at him. 'You must miss her. Your son, too.'

The Englishman tended to characterise his situation as that of a man cut off, by politics and sectarian injustice, from love. And it was true, he *was* cut off from love. But also from those things in a family that are not love and yet are also love. The accommodations, nuisances, bickerings and small enmities of a shared life. When you are separated, you are separated from everything – the good, the bad, the indifferent; the significant and the trivial – in equal measure. He'd have liked to discuss this with Paul, but if he tried to explain himself in English he would sound like an imbecile.

So, in reply, he simply said: 'Yes, I miss them.'

When I am in my bed I wish you were with me. When I cook, I wish you were there to eat with me. When I shower, I wish I could hear you pissing into the toilet.

He does not wish she was with him, in this country. In this city. The words that are said to him – in the street, in the stairwell, on buses – he would not wish for them to be said to her. They are out there, now, shouting. Kids. Maybe nine, ten years old. The same age as his son. Before leaving, he told the boy never to hate the people who hate him. But he, himself, hates. He hates those who cause him to be here, and he hates those kids.

When he thinks of his family, he thinks of water. His only son, swimming and splashing. His wife's skin in the reflected light.

There is no sea here, in Leeds, and so the sunsets are not as beautiful as they are at home. The city has a river and a canal

but it isn't safe for him to walk beside them.

★

5

One of the inscriptions on the desk reads: 'Id rather be a paki than a turk.'

He understood the meaning, but not the sense. Paul explained that two Leeds fans had been stabbed to death in Istanbul a couple of years ago; that, in the minds of the people who wrote this sort of graffiti, a Paki is the lowest life form. But Turks are the lowest of the low, now. They have daubed 'Die Turky Scum' over his door. They have daubed 'Paki Go Home'.

People here think I am a Pakistani. They think I am Turkish.

Paul told him, too, about the trial of the two footballers after a Pakistani student – from Yorkshire, in fact, but 'a Paki' – was beaten up outside a nightclub. Kicked. Stamped on. Bitten in the face. Left for dead. The players were heroes, Paul said. Not because of what happened, but because of who they were. Leeds players. England players. Our boys. Even those who were appalled by what was done to the student still stood up to shout Lee Bowyer's name, to celebrate his goals.

'Bowyer got off, in the end,' Paul said, 'but we didn't know that at the time.'

In describing the episode, Paul uses the student's name. Stressing it. Sarfraz Najeib. He has a name, he is a person, a human being. Once you know a man's name you cannot wish to harm him. This is what he imagines Paul believes. Or perhaps it is simply another subtlety in Paul's efforts to make it clear that he isn't a racist. This, he has noticed, is one of the differences between liberal intellectuals here and at home.

My tutor bought me a map of our country. The map is out of date, but I have put it up in the living room all the same so that Paul will see it whenever he visits. You wouldn't believe how they spell the name of our town!

He suspects that the Englishman is as lonely as he is.

Sometimes, he hears the kids chanting: 'LeeBow-yer! LeeBow-yer! LeeBow-yer!', the syllables echoing along the walkway; before Paul's explanation, he had no idea what the words meant, or why they chose his door at which to chant them.

★

'What would happen to you?' Paul had once asked.

He had shrugged.

'Would they put you in prison?' Then, after a moment's hesitation: 'Would you be tortured? Killed? Executed?'

'I don't know,' he'd said.

In between their meetings, Paul must spend time reading about his country and the situation there. The tutor presses this new expertise upon him whenever he can; he even manages an approximate pronunciation of the names of people and places. There is something proprietorial about this, something inveigling and, yet, oddly touching. He suspects that if he said he'd once been subjected to experiments on board a UFO, Paul would nod attentively and go away to gen up on alien-abduction theory.

On evenings when Leeds are playing, I like to stand at my window and look at the stadium, incandescent in the floodlights. It is a scene from a science fiction movie.

If he opens the window the noise of the crowd reaches him. Forty thousand voices. It is conceivable that, if he listened carefully for the entire ninety minutes, he could guess the score from the nature of their cries.

They have been playing tonight – they lost, he heard the result on his radio – and even though he has only watched them once (and is, in any case, a Man U fan) he is disappointed. He watches the spectators stream away from the ground, many of them filing across the park directly beneath his flats. Some of them are eating food from the take-away shop he himself has used; he can see the wrappers, ghostly white against their dark figures. The cars on the elevated section of motorway are nose-to-tail all the way into the city centre. Overhead, the clatter of a helicopter.

No news yet. But I remain confident. And, once I have permission to stay, it won't be long before you'll both be able to join me.

In the morning he will receive a letter informing him that the decision has been deferred, again.

In the morning, when he collects the letter from the mat, he will discover the arson attack. A lighted, petrol-soaked rag will have been pushed into letter-box while he slept and burnt itself into black scraps. The door will be scorched and blistered and there will be smoke stains on the ceiling, that is all. This will not be so bad. Not as bad as the times when there has been dog mess to clear up, or when the kids – if it is them – have urinated through the flap. He will open the door to assess the extent of the external damage, and there will be fresh graffiti.

Paul will be outraged. The Englishman will implore him to go to the police, the newspapers. To let them take photographs. But he will do none of this. And when Paul demands to know why, he will tell him that, in the circumstances, it is best not to agitate or to have his name associated with trouble or to risk provoking them further.

These are matters he understands from experience and which Paul, for all his reading, cannot begin to.

In the morning, he will compose another fragment of unsent letter:

I like it here. I have been made welcome, as I'm sure you will be. And there are many children living nearby for our son to play with.

But all of this is to come. For now, he is content to smoke a cigarette and, from his vantage point above the city, watch the Leeds fans heading for home.

My Soul to Keep

She rolls onto her left side, towards the camera. I note the time – 03:12:57. Strands of hair are snagged between her lips; a bare foot has emerged from the duvet and peers over the edge of the bed like a periscope. She swallows, crinkles her nose. As always, she smiles her Mona Lisa smile. According to the readings she is in REM, but her eyelids barely flicker.

Sleeping Beauty, the tabloids call her.

Even in the greenish night-vision lighting, Charlotte's features are flawless. It's easy to see why she captivates so many people. When she is facing the camera, I could gaze at the monitor for hours. When she turns away, I long for her to turn back. Awake, she never struck me as beautiful. Her grey eyes were almost always dull, her mouth a thin stripe that scarcely moved when she spoke. If you ask me, though, her beauty, her hypnotic appeal, isn't physical – it arises from her apparent serenity. She looks perfectly at peace with herself.

Dr Aziz tells us not to 'project'. But what alternative is there, with Charlotte?

I search her face for the faintest sign that she is aware – subliminally, unconsciously – of today's significance. Of course not. All I would see, if I saw anything, is the reflection of my own awareness. To Charlotte, it's simply one more night followed by one more day; although even that distinction is lost on her. She sleeps, she smiles. That's all.

The first time we met, she was just another patient. This was fifteen months ago.

Dr Aziz brought her along to the lab around 8.30pm. 'Charlotte, this is Kim, one of our Sleep Technicians,' he said. 'She'll be looking after you tonight.'

The girl's 'Hey' was so automatic I wondered if she'd understood why we were being introduced. She wore a blue T-shirt that said FUN in big yellow letters, ripped jeans and green converse; her straight, dark hair hung to her shoulders and looked unwashed.

'You at uni, Charlotte?' I asked, once it was the two of us. We were sitting in easy chairs in a corner of the lab while I filled in the paperwork. I knew she was a student; I was making conversation to relax her. It took more questions to get her to say which university, which course. 'Oh, one of my sons is there. Sam. But he's in his final year, so you –'

'Do I go to sleep now?' she said, eyeing the bed as if noticing it for the first time.

I set my pen down. Went over the procedure which Dr Aziz had already explained to her: the acclimatisation period; the attaching of the clips and electrodes.

'You'll go to bed about ten.'

From her appalled expression, I might have told her she had to stay up all night.

Charlotte had presented with depression near the end of her first semester at uni and was referred to her GP by student counselling, then to a Cognitive Behavioural Therapist. There'd been issues with anxiety and an eating disorder when she was fifteen but, this time, the indicators suggested the onset of a Major Depressive Episode. Depressed mood for most of the day: tick; markedly diminished interest or pleasure in all activities most of the day: tick; psychomotor retardation: tick; fatigue or loss of energy: tick; diminished ability to think or concentrate: tick; feelings of worthlessness: tick; thoughts of her own death: tick. Less typically, the symptoms included heightened appetite and increased eating – which should have provided a clue to the particular nature of her depression. 'Excessive sleep' had been noted as well, but her doctor hadn't probed any further into that. It was her CBT therapist who realised Charlotte had a serious sleep disorder, as well as a serious mood disorder – and that the two might be interrelated. She referred her to a specialist: Dr Aziz.

'Why are there so many clips and stuff?' Charlotte asked, that first evening.

I talked her through the function of each attachment: brain activity, eye movement, muscle activity, heart rhythm, breathing function, blood-oxygen level... I might have been hypnotising her, the way her eyelids drooped. 'Don't worry – you'll get used to them.'

'They won't keep me awake?'

I couldn't help laughing. 'They'd be pretty pointless if they did.'

'Uh, yeah. I guess.'

She looked so lost in her confusion. I hadn't warmed to her up to that point. I can't say I exactly warmed to her then, but I glimpsed her vulnerability. When you see the person inside the patient, you can't help noticing the person inside your professional self. *What if she was my daughter?* I recall thinking that, as I prepped her. Not that I have a daughter.

'I'm liking the pyjamas, by the way.'

She looked down at herself, as if trying to figure out why she was wearing pyjamas at all, or how they came to be patterned with tiny snowflakes. Like stars in a purple sky. 'Will you be watching me the whole time?' she asked.

'I'll be in the next room, yes. There's a monitor.' I indicated the camera. 'But I'll mainly be keeping track of the data feeds and making sure –'

'It's okay. I mean, I won't even know, will I?' She yawned, raised a hand to her mouth. Her pyjama sleeve slid down her forearm, the veins startlingly blue beneath the pale skin. 'You could draw glasses and a moustache on my face and I'd have no idea.'

She was asleep in four minutes; fast, but not untypical in hypersomnia. Nor was I all that surprised by the difficulty in waking her the next morning. The real sign that she was a special case came with the Polysomnography. Everyone, even a hypersomniac, is technically awake at numerous points during a period of sleep – a few seconds here, a few seconds there. But analysis across the range of PSG measurements showed this wasn't true for Charlotte. She slept for nine hours, eleven minutes without waking once, even for a nanosecond.

03:47:09. Security messages me: Charlotte's mother requests admittance, will I authorise? I authorise. She isn't due till ten, for the press conference, but I can imagine that she would want to sneak in early rather than cross a picket line of camera crews and photographers. I listen for her footsteps in the corridor. I don't appreciate company at work. That's why I've been on the late shift for the past two or so years, since Sam went to university. I'd rather be alone through the night, here, than at home in an empty house. People ask if I'm ever lonely, but there's a difference between loneliness and solitude.

In the doorway, I conjure a smile. 'Hello, Evelyn.'

She steps into the observation room, pink-cheeked from the cold night air, her black coat glittery with rain. Her hair is as dark as Charlotte's but chopped into a severe bob and threaded with grey. 'I couldn't sleep,' she says. Realising what she has said, she laughs, a little too loudly. 'God, that's ironic, isn't it?'

Has she been drinking? 'Actually, it's paradoxical. Not ironic.'

Evelyn blinks at me.

'Sorry,' I say. 'My ex was an English teacher.'

I detect a flinch at 'ex'. You'd think it would be a point of connection; but, whereas I've been divorced for five years, she's been separated from Charlotte's father for six months. We orbit the same planet but on different parabolas. I suspect the real problem between us, though, is that I spend more time with her daughter than she does. Evelyn shrugs off her coat but remains standing, one hand on the chair I've wheeled out for her. With a vague gesture in the direction she's just come from, she says, 'There are more of them tonight.'

She must be referring to the Sleep Camp across the street. 'Yeah,' I reply, 'some new ones were arriving when I came in.' This is their solstice, I suppose. Behind the barriers, in their makeshift bivouacs, Charlotte's devotees will sleep with her – as close as they can, anyway – as the final hours and minutes of her 365th day tick down.

'Can I sit with her?' Evelyn asks. In the lab, she means. 'Please, Kim.'

I should refuse permission. I should remind her, politely but firmly, that we're outside the agreed visiting hours – that I'm prepared to let her stay with me in the observation room, but that's all. *Dr Aziz will have my guts for garters*, I should say. What I say, instead, is:

'Come on, I'll take you through.'

The morning following her first PSG, Charlotte remained sleep-drunk for some time after I managed to wake her. Even a shower and a change of clothes didn't lift the drowsiness and disorientation. I wondered how much longer she would have slept if I'd just left her there. Her notes indicated that, at home, she was typically asleep by 9pm and awake by 8am, if uninterrupted. During the days, she would have naps, totalling 5–6 hours. But patients are unreliable at self-recording, often conflating Total Sleep Time with Time In Bed. Just as insomniacs can overestimate how much they're awake, so some hypersomniacs exaggerate their propensity for sleep. Not Charlotte. She understood her sleep architecture only too well.

'Would you like some breakfast?' I asked.

I might've been speaking Chinese for all the response I got. I ordered toast and cereal. By the time it arrived, Charlotte had come round. As we ate, I outlined the day ahead. The Multiple Sleep Latency Test: At two-hour intervals, she would be asked to go back to sleep, enabling us to profile her 'onset' – or how long she took to drop off. In between these times, she'd be given various boring, repetitive tasks to assess how easy or difficult it was for her to remain awake while performing them.

'This will be with one of my colleagues. I go off-shift at eight.'

'You work 12-hour shifts?' Charlotte bit into a triangle of toast.

'Four days on, three days off, yeah.'

Still chewing, she said, 'Just watching people sleep.'

'Or not sleeping. Most of our patients are insomniacs.'

'Isn't it boring?'

'As a Sleep Technician, it kind of goes with the territory.' The previous evening, she hadn't been remotely conversational. Already, I think I was aware that such moments of sociability – of normality – were, in fact, abnormal. For her. 'What about you?' I kept my tone light, teasing. 'Don't you get bored spending so much time asleep?'

'No.' Emphatic. Her mouth was lip-glossed with marmalade, but she either didn't realise or didn't care. 'Being *awake* –' she started to say, then stopped.

I tried to mask my interest. Weetabix, a sip of juice. Then, 'Being awake, what?'

But this young woman had done the rounds of counsellors, doctors, therapists; she saw me coming a mile off. 'Shouldn't Dr Aziz be the one to ask those sorts of questions?'

On the monitor, Evelyn positions a chair at her daughter's bedside and sits down. She knows not to hold Charlotte's hand, or stroke her hair, or kiss her, but sits close enough to do all of those things, if she chose to. She visits four or five times a week but, because I work lates, her dealings are usually with the day team. Occasionally, she'll arrive as I go off-shift, or leave as I turn up. Three times, she has come at night to sit with me in the observation room; but the last of these nocturnal visits was months ago. She has never asked to enter the sleep-lab itself out of visiting hours. Until tonight.

She's talking to Charlotte; softly, but the mic picks up every word. My colleagues have told me about this: the long, chatty monologues, sometimes punctuated by weeping or pleas for her daughter to wake up. Dr Aziz has forbidden all non-clinical physical contact in case it interferes with the PSG channels, but he relaxed the rules on 'noise disturbance' when it became evident that Charlotte is entirely unresponsive to aural stimuli. Whether it's the bed-bath nurse dropping a stainless-steel bowl on the floor or Evelyn murmuring in her daughter's ear, the graphs remain stubbornly, relentlessly unaffected.

I mute the volume to grant her some privacy. And because I can't bear to hear it.

I speak to Charlotte myself at times: when I enter the lab to replace a dislodged attachment, or to adjust the feeding tube, or IV, or catheter, or simply to cover her when the bedclothes go walkabout. *Just clipping this back on your finger, Charlotte,* or *Let's tuck you in, shall we?* That sort of thing. Other stuff as well, if I'm honest.

'People in a coma can hear voices,' Evelyn once said to me.

Of course, Charlotte isn't in a vegetative state – she's asleep, not comatose. Cerebral and neurological functions are normal; there has been no brain trauma, or infection, or other identifiable cause for her unresponsiveness. Remarkably, it seems she put herself to sleep, and keeps herself asleep. It's inexplicable, but nothing we've tried – cold plunge-baths, loud bangs, loud music, pin-pricks, epidermal vibration, mild

15

shocks, stimulants, bright light – has brought that sleep to an end. Yet it's conceivable that she might wake herself at any moment.

I watch Evelyn, watching her daughter.

When Will had pneumonia, I sat at his bedside through the night. It's what mums do. He sent me a photo-message yesterday – a selfie, with Angkor Wat in the background; week 32 of his gap-year trip. No text, just the picture and a smiley emoticon. I stuck another pin in the map on the wall of his old bedroom. I've seen Charlotte's bedroom in the newspapers and on TV; Evelyn keeps it exactly as it was the day her daughter entered the clinic long-term.

Her lips are still moving. Charlotte is still facing her, facing me, but her foot has retreated beneath the covers. She sleeps, she smiles.

Where do you go to, my lovely? What thoughts surround you, alone in your bed?

A year ago, she was unwell, desperately unhappy. But her perpetually tranquil smile invites us to assume she is happy, now; that she has attained a Buddha-like state of bliss.

I didn't see Charlotte again for six weeks after that first time.

At home, under her mother's supervision, she followed the plan drawn up by Dr Aziz. For a specialist in cognitive behavioural therapy, he takes an eclectic position on the treatment of depression – happy to stir biological and psychoanalytical approaches into the mix, if needs be. *With a patient like Charlotte, we might have to throw the kitchen sink in.* So he prescribed a cocktail of stimulant and antidepressant drugs, a new diet, physical exercises, the keeping of a sleep diary, prohibition of sleep outside night-time hours, increased daytime activity and bright-light therapy. She also saw Dr Aziz once a week for CBT, designed to challenge her perceptions about sleep. Hypersomnia patients often believe the only way to feel less tired is to sleep more; they have to be helped to think differently. Text-book stuff. Except that the text books for hypersomnia with depression, or depression with hypersomnia, are a work-in-progress. All we knew, pre-Charlotte, was that hypersomnia is the single most treatment-resistant symptom in depression; and that studies showed you must treat the sleep disorder as well as the mood disorder to achieve the best results for both.

Charlotte didn't improve on either front in those six weeks. She deteriorated.

'The root of the problem,' Dr Aziz declared at a team briefing, 'is that she doesn't sleep in order to feel less tired.'

'Why does she, then?' I asked.

'That, Kim, is the million-dollar question.'

With her consent, she was readmitted; this time, she would be with us for a week. Unprecedented. Hideously expensive. But, even back then, it was apparent that Charlotte's case was unique, opening up a ground-breaking area of research. He's a fine clinician, Dr Aziz, but he's even better at writing funding bids.

We played Scrabble, the first evening; a ploy to keep her awake until bedtime. In the 11 hours between Charlotte's readmission and the start of my shift, she'd clocked up 7.4 hours in short sleeps. *Rapid onsets; significant difficulty reawakening*, the handover notes said. *Marked avolition and anergia when awake*. Lack of motivation; lack of energy. Or, as my ex once put it: 'can't be arsed' and 'still can't be arsed'. (This was in the days when he still showed an interest in my work; when I still found his cynicism amusing.)

'There are two l's in "fuelled",' Charlotte said, after I'd taken a turn.

'Yeah, but I only have one,' I said. She frowned, then realised I was joking – that I'd tried to cheat. 'You should smile more often,' I told her, changing it to 'fled'. 'It suits you.'

She blushed, lowered her gaze. We'd been playing for about 20 minutes and she had already come close to nodding off two or three times. On her goes, she put down any old word, clumsily, seemingly uninterested in how many points it scored.

'We could switch the TV on, if you'd rather. Or watch a DVD.'

Charlotte placed some letters. 'You don't have to be nice to me,' she said, as if talking to the Scrabble board. 'I get enough of that crap from my mum. And Dr Aziz.'

'*Dr Aziz?* He hasn't been "nice" to anyone since 2007.'

She didn't smile, or come close.

This was a typical conversation around that time. For me, at least. I gathered that Charlotte was even less forthcoming, less focused, with my colleagues – especially with Dr Aziz, on whom she had more or less shut down.

We were still unsure of the exact nature of her depression and its inter-relationship with her hypersomnia. Stress induced by the first-semester assessments at uni, social anxiety over living away from home and struggling to form friendships, the death of her grandmother the previous summer, the break-up with the boyfriend she'd had in sixth-form, losing her part-time job as a barista because she kept oversleeping and turning up late, the warning emails from her Progress Tutor about the number of lectures she'd missed, a bout of flu which wiped her out for most of the Christmas vacation... there was no shortage of potential contributory factors in her depressive episode. But why did she sleep so much? And why, despite all the treatment, was she sleeping more and more?

'Why won't you let anyone in, Charlotte?' I asked, as I wired her up. This would've been the fifth or sixth evening.

'I don't want to *talk* anymore.'

'We're on your side, you know. We want you to get better.'

'No you're not. And no you don't.'

'No?'

'What you want – all of you – is to stop me sleeping.'

'Aren't they two sides of the same coin, though? You sleep, you get depressed; you get depressed, you sleep.'

'Is that what you think?' She shoved her fingers through her hair as if she wanted to yank it out by the roots. 'Jesus Christ.'

'So, *tell* me Charlotte. Please. Tell me how it really –'

'You want me to be "happy", right?'

'Yes,' I said. 'Of course I do.'

'Then for fuck's sake let me *sleep*.' Her eyes filled with tears; her shoulders shook. 'When I'm asleep, all the bad stuff goes away. Don't you see that?'

That week, her Total Sleep Time increased day by day. She became more resistant to being woken, more sleep-drunk and uncommunicative in the brief interludes when she was awake. In the final 24-hour period before we discharged her, her daytime sleep totalled 9.1 hours; that night, she slept for 10.5. This defied the laws of physiology. Sleep is driven by homeostatic and circadian rhythms: the more we sleep, the harder it is *to* sleep. And hunger or thirst should wake us, at some point, or the urge to go to the toilet. Not so, with Charlotte.

Ten days later, Evelyn phoned the clinic to report that her daughter had just gone a full 24 hours without waking. She was an emergency admission, then: if she didn't wake up, she couldn't eat or drink by herself. She remained asleep in the ambulance; she remained asleep here, in the lab, hydrated by a drip and with a feeding tube inserted into her stomach. No matter what we did, she slept and slept.

A new medical condition had been identified: Persistent Hypersomnic State, or PHS.

Before long, the whole world would know Charlotte's name.

Across the road, they've started chanting. I go to the window and peer through the blinds. It's just after 5am; the sky is still dark but the Sleep Camp is bathed by street lights. There are three or four times the usual number of tents, wigwams and yurts. On a typical night, the regulars and long-termers remain zipped away inside, sleeping or maintaining a silent vigil; but this is not a typical night, and the newcomers appear to be in the majority. The devotees sit cross-legged wherever there's space on the pavement, facing the clinic, eyes closed as if in worship, or raised towards the blacked-out second-floor window of the sleep-lab. Some hold up lit candles or the illuminated screens of their phones.

Charlie, they chant. *Charlie, Charlie, Charlie.*

It must be loud if I can hear them up here. What do they hope or expect? That, on the first anniversary of her entry into PHS, Charlotte will pick this moment to wake up? That she'll appear miraculously at the window above them, like a Living Goddess in Kathmandu, and let them gaze upon her beatific face?

A TV camera crew is there already; a couple of photographers. The 'true sleepers' in the camp must hate this. The noise, the showiness. Those who have been there all along, or who return again and again, have one declared purpose: to sleep in sympathy and solidarity with Charlotte. If you ask me, it's more than that – they seek whatever they imagine she has; they long to be hypersomniacs, too.

I step away from the window. On the monitor, Evelyn no longer seems to be talking. She might even have fallen asleep herself, in the bedside chair. As for Charlotte, she is in non-REM now. She smiles, as always.

Charlie, Charlie.

The Sleep Camp materialised after the Channel 4 documentary, broadcast to mark her 100th day. One tent, at first. Two 19-year-old girls. All the campers – regulars and casuals – have been female, aged from 15 to 25. The under-18s are rooted out by the police or social services, or by their parents, and packed off home. *A Sleeping Beauty for the 21st*

Century, the programme was titled. Dr Aziz, with the consent of Charlotte's parents (still together at that stage), had allowed the film crew into the sleep-lab. A serious, intelligent documentary was the intention; but, on television, human interest trumps psychological research every time. Even while the film was on air, our medical phenomenon had become an internet and social media sensation. By the following day, Charlotte's face – that mesmerising smile – was everywhere. She was the lead story on every news bulletin, every front page and home page. She trended. The only thing anyone was talking, commenting, tweeting, 'liking' or trolling about. They loved her, they hated her; they pitied her, they blamed her; they accused her of faking it, they hailed her as a saint.

In the next few hours it will begin again, as the girl who has slept for a hundred days reaches another milestone: the girl who has slept for a year.

Not 'girl'; a young woman. Last month she 'celebrated' her twentieth birthday.

I log the data sets. It's what I do. What we do: round-the-clock Polysomnography, each 12-hour block of recorded information processed and analysed, every variation in the pattern and physiology of her sleep pored over for signs of change or clues to PHS. There never is any change, though. Charlotte's sleep is as remorseless, as featureless, as a desert.

At 05:41:22, I head along the corridor to the vending machine for my cappuccino fix. As the drink dispenses, the sleep-lab door opens and Evelyn emerges; groggy, distracted, her hair mussed up, she comes to join me.

'Can you hear them outside?' she asks, her voice raspy.

'Uh-huh.'

I expect her to make a disparaging remark about the Sleep Campers, or about the chanting, but, instead, she crumples into tears and I find myself enfolding her in my arms.

So, we had a rationale: When I'm asleep all the bad stuff goes away. And an implicit: If I wake up, the bad stuff comes back. That evening, more than a year ago – over a game of Scrabble – I coaxed a little more from Charlotte before she drifted into pre-sleep incoherence.

'What "bad stuff"?'

She rubbed her face, as if cross with herself for crying. 'Everything.'

I check-listed some of the issues we already knew about but she just shook her head to shut me up. If she slept to escape all of that, why would she want to talk about it?

'I *love* going to bed,' she said, instead. 'Snuggling under the duvet, letting my head sink into the pillow, closing my eyes.' Her Mona Lisa smile surfaced.

'The cosiness?' The womb-like warmth and comfort and security, I left unsaid.

'The emptiness,' she said.

'Emptiness?'

'I lie there and empty everything out of my head and the sleep takes it away.' Her intensity was startling. In that moment, it really mattered to her that I understood. But my next questions irritated her, broke the connection.

'Do you dream?'

I knew she must, from the phases of REM, but she shrugged and said, 'If I do, I never remember them.'

'Do you think happy thoughts, then? Picture yourself in a happy pl–'

'I. Just. Sleep.'

'But, Charlotte, you can't sleep all the time. Can't sleep away the rest of your life.'

She didn't answer. Her expression said it clearly enough: *Why can't I?*

When we discussed this conversation at the case conference, Dr Aziz hypothesised that Charlotte's sleep-craving was a surrogate death-impulse. With her previous therapist, she'd never spoken of feeling suicidal or considering ways to kill herself, as some depressives do. But she had wondered what it would be like to be dead.

'Can we infer,' Dr Aziz said, 'that Charlotte imagines death would be like sleeping?'

'The ultimate avoidance strategy?' one of the team suggested. 'All the time you're asleep, you don't have to *cope*. And if you're dead, or as good as, then you'll never –'

'Quite.' Dr Aziz managed a grim smile. 'There's a beautifully illogical logic to it.'

He would pursue that line in his consultations with Charlotte over the weeks ahead.

It never happened, of course. Within ten days of being discharged, and after only one further therapy session (in which she blanked him), Charlotte went into PHS. Just when we'd unearthed a reason for her hypersomnia, we had no hope of reasoning her out of it.

'She's always been headstrong,' Evelyn says. 'Stubborn.'

Another paradox: Charlotte lacks motivation and energy, yet has the force of will to self-induce a year's sleep. Standing by the vending machine, I say as much to her mother.

'That's why they chant her name,' she replies. 'They think she's so fucking heroic.'

Her anger catches me off-guard. Is she annoyed with Charlotte's devotees, or with Charlotte? Or both? 'I hadn't thought about it like that,' I say, trying to be neutral.

'When Charlie had her eating disorder, we found out that she'd been going on this website – *Thinspiration*.' Evelyn's face is still blotchy from crying, her eyelashes dewy. 'All those girls, with their ribcages and cheekbones. Now she's the one being idolised.'

I retrieve my cappuccino and step aside so she can take her turn at the machine. For all that we've just hugged, we are more awkward with one another, not less. She presses

'Americano'. The cup drops into the slot and starts to fill.

'How d'you think they would feel if she woke up?' I ask. 'The Sleep Campers.'

'Let down.' She removes the drink before it has finished dispensing, seemingly indifferent to the scalding liquid splashing her fingers. '*How dare she betray us by waking up?*' As if it follows on naturally, Evelyn asks, 'You have children don't you, Kim?'

'Well, children – they're 23 and 21. Boys.' I tell her their names, and what they're doing now. She gazes along the corridor towards the door to the lab.

I break off. 'You ready to be swiped back in?'

'Do you miss them?' she asks. 'Your boys.'

'Ah, well. They have their own lives to –'

'I miss Charlie terribly, that's the thing. I want her to wake up for *my* sake as much as hers.' She turns back towards me, searching my face. 'Is that selfish of me?'

I hold her gaze. 'No, I wouldn't say it was.'

She nods but looks unconvinced. We walk back along the corridor with our coffees and stand together by the sleep-lab door. Through the viewing panel I see that Charlotte has turned over, away from us; her hair is draped across the pillow like a black silk scarf.

'How are you feeling about the press conference?' I ask.

'Oh, you know.'

I don't. I have no idea. The light on the security pad blinks from red to green as the door unlocks. I hold it ajar. She pauses, one hand splayed beside mine on the blonde wood; her long, thin fingers next to my stubby ones, we make a bird with asymmetrical wings.

Evelyn says. 'I'll be notifying Dr Aziz this morning, so you might as well know.'

'Notifying him?'

We are speaking in lowered voices, conditioned to being quiet around someone who's asleep, even when it's Charlotte.

Evelyn takes the weight of the door, her knuckles whitening, but I leave my hand where it is all the same.

'I'm withdrawing Charlie,' she says. 'I'm taking her home.'

A few days ago, on my cappuccino break, instead of returning to the observation room, I went into the lab. I sat with Charlotte for an hour. Sixty-three minutes, five seconds, to be exact. It would've taken some explaining if Dr Aziz had chosen that time to review the AV rather than simply reading the reports. The anniversary was looming – that might've been a factor; we were all in a state of heightened awareness. Also, I hadn't heard from Will or Sam in about ten days. Not that that's unusual, or any excuse for being so unprofessional.

'In the first few weeks after my marriage broke up – after he left me – I dreaded going to bed at night.' That was one of the things I told her. 'The boys were both still at home, then, or I'd have slept in one of their rooms. So, what I did was sleep on top of the duvet, in a sleeping bag. Like he'd died and I couldn't bear to be in the space we'd shared for all those years, smelling him on the bedding no matter how often it went through the wash.'

On it went, my monologue. Pouring out of me. I'd never told anyone any of it.

How poorly I slept when I did finally drag myself to bed; how, perversely, I couldn't face getting up in the mornings. What was the point? Will and Sam, of course. But for them, I'd have lain in that sleeping bag half the day, not sleeping. Hating myself.

'Do you hate yourself, Charlotte?' I asked. 'I mean, *did* you, before this? Because you can't hate yourself when you're asleep, can you?'

Naturally, she didn't respond. I swept the hair from her face. Her forehead was cool and dry. Even once I'd withdrawn my hand I felt the ghost of her skin on my fingertips.

I can't recall everything I said to her in that hour,

between the silences when I merely stared at her face. But I remember this: I sang to her. 'Scarborough Fair'. I used to sing it to the boys, when they were little, to soothe them to sleep. Now, I was singing it to Charlotte: a lullaby for the incessant sleeper. I swear that her eyelids flickered and her smile widened.

Afterwards, back in the observation room, I was convinced the graphs would show a momentary awakening that coincided with the singing. But, nothing. The whole time I'd sat with her, she had slept as deeply, as soundly, as ever.

Dr Aziz's office reeks of Evelyn's perfume. He has told me what I already knew, what he has only just heard himself.

'Can she do that?' I ask him across the desk.

'Why couldn't she? Charlotte has only ever been here with her mother's consent.'

I know that. Of course I do. I must be the least of Dr Aziz's priorities, just now, but he spares me the time even so. Evelyn, he explains, has raised enough money (by re-mortgaging the house, by signing a deal with a newspaper) to pay for her daughter to receive proper care at home for 18 months. Staff have been hired, preparations made. Charlotte's sleep will no longer be monitored. She'll be fed and hydrated, bathing and toilet will be attended to, along with regular medical checks. That's all. From now on, she sleeps in her own bed, in her own bedroom, until she wakes up. Whenever that might be.

'What about me?' The question is out before I can stop myself.

Dr Aziz frowns. 'Take a week off, Kim,' he says. 'Go somewhere nice. I'll have a new patient for you by the time you come back.'

I leave the clinic by the rear exit to avoid the press and the Sleep Camp. The walk to the bus-stop, the bus ride... none of it registers. But I find myself at the front door, letting myself into the house. It must've rained because my coat and hair are damp. I go through to the kitchen, only to stand in the middle of the room as if I've forgotten what I came in here for.

Breakfast, that's it. My routine after a shift: eat breakfast, take a shower, change into my pyjamas, close the bedroom curtains, read in bed till I'm ready to sleep.

I can't face breakfast this morning. Or any of it.

In the lounge, I slump on the sofa. I message Sam and Will. Sam won't be up, unless he has a morning lecture; maybe not even then. As for Will... I try to calculate the time in Cambodia but the maths is beyond me. I set the phone down on the coffee table. I'm still wearing my coat, I realise. At the clinic, the press conference will take place shortly. I picture the journalists assembling; Dr Aziz and Evelyn, in an ante-room, having clip-mics attached while a make-up person powders their faces for the cameras.

In the lab, Charlotte sleeps.

I imagine the day team will have already removed all of the clips and electrodes and switched off the monitoring equipment. Later on, someone will detach the feeding tube, the IV, the catheter; they will bathe her, dress her, brush her hair. Then she'll be taken home and her bed will be empty.

For a time, I simply sit on the sofa. It seems like only a few minutes have passed but, according to my phone, it's 10:37. I must have dozed off. But I don't feel as though I have. Whatever, I take off my coat and hang it on one of the hooks by the front door, then fetch my bag into the lounge. I remove the large envelope containing the discs I brought home from work and select one at random. The remote isn't anywhere obvious, so I have to kneel on the floor in front of the TV and activate the DVD player manually. The tray slides out. I insert the disc and it slides in again. My knees click as I stand up and return to the sofa. The cushions are damp, but that doesn't matter.

After a moment, the screen flickers into life and her image appears.

She is lying on her left, eyes closed, face turned towards the camera. Smiling at me.

Because of Olsen

STIRRED BY VOICES, MILLER awoke in an unfamiliar room. At first it was the morning-pale surroundings that disorientated him. On his back, stupid with unshed sleep, he failed to make sense of the ceiling (high, corniced), the cast of light from the window (left to right), and the garish, too-thin curtains rucked to a halt on an ancient radiator. But the book on the bedside table was the one he had been reading the night before, and there were his phone, his wallet, his keys. With them, came the recollection of where he was. As these details resolved themselves the talking reclaimed his attention, became the new point of disorientation. There had been several voices before, but now there was just one – male, nasal, slightly camp – coming from the landing. Another of the tenants, he supposed, or callers at a neighbouring bedsit. Miller rolled over to stare at the door, straining to hear what was being said beyond it. At that moment, a key turned in the lock, the door opened, and a group of people – perhaps as many as ten – filed into the room to form a cramped semi-circle facing his bed, where he lay, naked and partially covered. One of them, a tall, sporty blonde, aimed a camera and took his picture.

Once they'd all filed back out, and Miller had slung on some clothes, the guy with the nasal voice re-entered alone, knocking this time. He was in his early twenties, student-ish, his head variously pierced.

'What are you doing here?' he said.

Miller was still buttoning his shirt. 'I live here.'

'I mean, what are you doing *in*?'

'Why am I *in* the room I live in?'

From the other guy's expression, the point of the question eluded him. Miller rubbed his face with his hand. 'Okay, let's start this conversation over again, only this time I'm the one who gets to say: "What are you doing here?"' He was conscious of sounding like a character in an inferior American sitcom.

'It's 10am,' the student-type said.

'Jesus.' Miller needed coffee, food, a shower. No longer looking at the other guy but at the floor between them, he said: 'Uh-huh, 10am. Tell me about 10am.'

'The last guy, he used to just clear out for half an hour.'

'The tenant before me?'

'Luke something.'

'And why would he do that?'

'While I showed the Danes round.'

'Danes.' Miller glanced at the door. He could hear their voices, out on the landing. 'Those people are Danish?'

'One of them's Norwegian, I think. Bergen. Is that Norway?'

Miller gave him a look. 'Let me get this straight. At 10am, I clear out of my bedsit for half an hour while you bring the Danes in. Is that how it goes?'

'Only on Saturdays.'

He shifted into sitcom-speak again. 'And I do this, *be-cause...*?'

'That's when Mr Kaursar said they could come.'

Miller exhaled. 'What I'm trying to clarify... sorry, what's your name?'

'Ben.'

'The point I'm trying to clarify, Ben, is this: Why do a bunch of fucking Danes get to come into my fucking bedsit at 10am. every fucking Saturday?'

'Because of Olsen.'

Ben was right, there was a clause in the tenancy agreement – which Miller had signed without reading – permitting London Art Tours Ltd. to enter the building, and Miller's bedsit in particular, on Saturday mornings. No, the Mr Kaursar hadn't thought to mention it when they'd discussed the lease; he was sorry, but... Miller pictured the moustachioed smile, the waggle of the head. The rent, it was pointed out, had been adjusted to compensate for any inconvenience – and the tours had been running all summer, without complaint from the previous tenant. As for this Olsen character, the landlord knew nothing of him, beyond what was inscribed on the plaque outside. Hadn't Miller noticed the blue plaque?

As soon as he was done talking to Mr Kaursar, Miller shut off his phone, slung his copy of the tenancy agreement back in a drawer and – jostling through the party of Danes, and one Norwegian, still gathered on the landing – went out into the street. There it was, high up on the wall above the front-door lintel:

Thorvald Olsen
(1884–1914)

Artist lived and painted here
from September 1912 to March 1914

Miller was surprised not to have noticed the plaque when he had come to view the bedsit, and again, yesterday, when he'd moved in. Olsen had died at thirty, the age Miller was now. He thought about that – and about 1914, wondering whether he'd been killed in the First World War, but unsure if the Danes had taken part.

Miller returned to a deserted staircase and landing. The tour party was back inside his room, attending to their guide's nasal, slightly camp, monologue.

'... at his most prolific and innovative, producing some of his best...'

Miller's reappearance effected a pause. Every face turned his way. He caught the eye of the woman who'd taken his photograph, then found himself trying to figure out which of them was the Norwegian, and whether it might be her. Ben, occupying what little space there was between the group and the unmade bed, tugged at his triple-pierced earlobe and looked at Miller as though nervous of another outburst. In fact, seeing them all like that, engrossed in the guide's spiel, Miller felt as if he was the intruder, now. Instead of telling them, for the second time that morning, to piss off out of his room, he coughed, lowered his eyes and apologised for interrupting. With that, Miller collected his keys and wallet from the bedside table, excused himself again and left, pulling the door closed with a soft click. He would clear out for half an hour, find some place serving fresh coffee and all-day breakfast and wait for the Danes to leave.

As it happened, one of them – the blonde, with the camera – had stayed behind.

The sex was as athletic as Miller had imagined, although he had the vague sense of being, if not surplus to requirements, incidental to the woman's pleasure. He mentioned this afterwards, as they lay in bed, not smoking.

'It is the room,' she said. 'Olsen's room.'

'You were fucking the room?'

'I was fucking *in* the room. The room where Olsen worked. On *his* bed.'

Not the actual bed, Miller hoped. Not the mattress, at least. But, then, with Mr Kaursar, anything was conceivable. 'Who was this Olsen?'

She lifted her head from the pillow to look at him. 'You're not serious.'

Her English was excellent, if a little mannered. 'I don't know much about art,' Miller said. Danish art, he meant. 'I take it he's famous in Denmark, then?'

The woman had a scar in the centre of her forehead – like the third eye of Hinduism, only white – but her face was otherwise unblemished, tanned and perfect. Miller had never fathomed how Scandinavians, who had two weeks of daylight a year, always looked so honey-skinned. She frowned and the scar disappeared. 'What is the word for someone who is not famous everywhere but is followed by some people?'

'A cult figure,' Miller suggested.

'Exactly. That is Olsen. A *cult figure.*'

'In Denmark.'

'Of course in Denmark. And a little in Norway. People who like Munch, also they like Olsen.' She flapped a hand in front of her face, as she might have done if they had been sharing a cigarette and the smoke was bothering her. 'This is the last years, only. Olsen was nothing much for a long time and now he is having a...'

'Revival?'

'Renaissance.'

Miller turned the difference over in his mind: brought back to life, born again. He wasn't sure which he preferred; if you were dead, he supposed, you'd settle for either if it meant a kind of immortality. Or maybe not. What did he know about death? Miller shifted to make himself more comfortable beside her in the narrow bed.

'So, what sort of stuff did he paint?'

'It is not possible to describe. You must see for yourself.'

'Okay, why do you like him so much?'

The woman considered this. 'He paints the soul.'

'The human soul?'

'His own. All great painters can see inside their soul. When Olsen paints he looks inside his own soul.' She hesitated. Miller couldn't tell if she was working out what to say or debating whether to say it. At last, so quietly he barely heard the words: 'And when I look at Olsen's soul... I see inside mine.'

Miller smiled. 'I like that.'

'This is what makes the great painter into a genius,' she said, flatly. They lay there in silence for a time after that. Miller thought he might be in love with her, but decided he didn't much like her and was in fact in love with the moment. The woman – he didn't know her name, he realised – sat up and asked to use the bathroom.

'Are the others in there?' Miller said.

'Others?'

'The rest of your tour party.'

She frowned again. 'Why would they be in your bathroom?'

Miller shook his head, told her it didn't matter. He'd found that the Dutch shared a similar sense of humour with the English and, for no logical reason, he'd thought the Danes might, too. But they didn't. At least, not this one. He knew then, if he hadn't already – if the fact of this being Olsen's room, Olsen's bed, Olsen's fuck, hadn't made it evident – that, after she left, they would never see one another again.

'What is your job?' she said, pointedly, as though the answer might explain his strange remark about the bathroom.

'I'm an actor,' he replied, despite having not auditioned or performed in almost a year. What he *did* was work part-time in a call centre – but that wasn't what he *was*. Miller figured that so long as you described yourself as an actor, you remained one.

'Really?' She seemed almost interested. 'What kind of acting?'

'TV, mostly. And a bit of theatre.' This was true. Had been true. 'I'm not in anything just now.'

The woman nodded. 'Of course, or why do you live in this shit-dump?'

Other people's passions aren't always infectious, or even interesting, and Miller found the woman's implacable belief in Olsen's genius irritating, given that hardly anyone outside Denmark had heard of him. Nevertheless, mulling over the encounter, he was drawn back to that tremulous hush when she'd spoken of seeing into her soul. Even as he doubted whether it was possible, or desirable, Miller imagined what that revelation would be like. And what work of art might be so evocative, so disturbing, as to make you believe you had peered into the core of your being. It was this, more than the fact of living in the long-dead painter's long-abandoned lodgings, that aroused Miller's curiosity. In the days that followed, he set about uncovering what he could of Olsen.

Miller had sold his laptop when the call centre reduced his hours and his phone was old, un-smart. So, he hit an internet café. There were websites devoted to Olsen – text in Danish, translations in gobbledegook – but none of the thumbnails would enlarge. And although there was a recently opened permanent exhibition in Århus, the gallery's website was still under construction. He looked up London Art Tours, but Olsen was simply listed among the artists in their walks programme. Even an online encyclopaedia of European modern art contained no images of his work, just a biographical sketch.

Olsen, Thorvald (1884-1914), b. Århus, Denmark. Expressionist painter. Early works (e.g. *Cathedral of St Clement*, 1908; *Seascape, Kattegat*, 1909) betrayed a derivative cubist influence. In 1910, Olsen moved to Dresden, attracted by the early experiments in what was to become Expressionism. Principal works from this period: *Point of Self*, 1910; *Ich*, 1911; and an untypically surrealist parody of Vermeer, *Pearl with a Girl Earring*, 1912.) After a dispute with his mentor, Ernst Ludwig Kirchner, he moved to London in 1912, where, in the eighteen months to his death, he produced what are considered to be his finest pieces (e.g. *Self-Portrait as an Animal*, 1912; *Disaffection in Blue and Red, 1913*; *Yellow Dawn, with Man at Window*, 1913; *The Roof*, 1914; *Transcendence*, 1914.) His later work is characterised by striking use of colour and formal dislocation. In its recurrent thematic, it is redolent of the solipsistic, baleful angst of Edvard Munch's *The Scream*, and prefigures by forty years the nihilistic pessimism of Francis Bacon. Olsen killed himself on March 18th, 1914, his thirtieth birthday.

'Did it happen in this room?' Miller said.

The guide was doing that thing with his earlobe. 'No,' he said.

'It did, didn't it?'

'No, it really didn't.'

Miller had planned on intercepting Ben the following Saturday, as the next tour arrived. The idea of living in the very room where the artist topped himself had taken hold. He was unsure how people committed suicide in those days – hanging?, a pistol shot to the head?, an overdose of laudanum? – but, whatever the method, he saw his lodgings in a new light. After all this time, even the most sophisticated 21st century forensics wouldn't find the minutest trace of Olsen's death. All the same, and as if some physical residue – some stain, odour or fragment – had lingered undetected all this time, Miller was acutely conscious of the man's presence, as he hadn't been before. There was an atmosphere, now. He would speak to that guy Ben about it. In the event, he hadn't had to wait till Saturday – on Friday evening, as he ate chicken jalfrezi straight from the carton, Miller answered a knock at the door to find the tour guide standing where the delivery guy had stood just a few minutes earlier.

'No, don't tell me,' Miller said, 'on Fridays, it's Swedes and Finns.'

'I just wanted to check you were cool for tomorrow.'

'Shipping myself out of here at 10am, you mean?'

'Only, what happened last week – that was just too embarrassing.'

Miller let that remark slide. Instead, he shifted the conversation into the exchange about Olsen's suicide. Miller disbelieved him when he insisted it hadn't taken place in the bedsit, but Ben wouldn't be pressed. This was where Olsen painted, he said – *that* was what brought the Danes here.

'Have you seen his work?' Miller said.

'Yeah, sure.'

'And?'

He gave a shrug. 'I prefer Kokoschka, myself. Or Soutine.'

The names meant nothing to Miller. They were still in the doorway and he became aware just then that he'd been holding a strip of garlic naan the whole time. He wanted to go back to his meal, but if he sent Ben away now he would let slip the chance to find out more about Olsen. So he invited him in, divided the remaining food between two plates and broke open another beer. The guide's piercings (ears, nose, lip, eyebrow) glinted in the light like splinters of Morse code.

'I'm guessing you're a student?'

He nodded, chewing. 'UCL. Art History.'

'That figures,' Miller said. 'The Olsen tours, I mean.'

'Olsen, Bacon, Hockney. I do Wyndham Lewis and the Vorticists as well.' He ate some more. From the way he shovelled the food down, you'd have thought he hadn't eaten in a week. 'The landlady here was a friend of Lewis's. In Olsen's time, yeah? It was a kind of hostel for struggling young artists, this place.'

Ben's T-shirt, bright red with yellow text, said: *Ceci n'est pas un T-shirt.* The jalfrezi was done and they were on to their second beer before Ben, who'd been hunched over the plate as though it was an examination paper, eased back into his chair. A companionable silence followed. Miller, having been alone since the split with Kate six months before, saw that this was how it would be to live with someone again. The thought made him acutely conscious of his loneliness. He pictured Olsen, in this same small room, relentlessly pessimistic, beset with baleful angst; working right up to the end, though. The last two paintings were dated 1914, which meant he completed them in the final weeks of his life. Miller, for whom the *inability* to work – to act – was the route to despondency, tried to comprehend how such a surge of artistic self-expression could co-exist with the despair that drove Olsen to kill himself.

He asked what Ben knew of Olsen. The guide riffed his weekly spiel to the Danes, but it added little to what Miller himself had found out; no insights into his mental state towards the end. *Suicidal,* was Ben's guess. Despite Olsen's resurgent popularity, no biography had been written, as yet, and even the gallery dedicated to him in his home town could barely dig up enough on the man to fill a leaflet.

'No-one's even sure what he looked like.'

'No photos?'

'Nada.'

'Where can I get to see his paintings?' Miller said. 'Apart from Århus.'

'We had a load of posters and prints and stuff shipped over.' Ben drained his beer. 'You can order online. Londonarttoursdotsomething.' He looked at his empty plate and shrugged. 'Or I can drop some off tomorrow.'

'The ones he did when he was living here?'

'Uh-huh, whatever.'

With that, the guide said he had to be someplace else, and stood up to leave. Miller's next question halted him at the door. 'Where *did* he do it, Ben?'

He hesitated, looked at Miller as though deciding whether he was fit to be told. Finally, he pointed to the ceiling. 'He jumped.'

'From the roof?'

Ben gave a simple nod. Neither of them spoke for a moment. Then he opened the door to let himself out, turning to gesture at the bed, the room in general. 'Oh, and, like, if it could be a bit *tidier* this time, yeah?'

You couldn't go up on the roof any more. Miller tried at first light the next day. On the fourth-floor landing, just along from the fire-escape, a small set of steps ended at what might once have been a trap-door but which had long since been filled in and crudely plastered. The fire-escape door itself opened on to a flight of iron stairs that zigzagged down to a yard at the rear of the building. Above, the edge of the flat roof was a metre or more out of reach. Miller stood out there for a while in the early chill, gazing up, then went back inside and pulled the door shut.

That was the starting point.

To begin with, Miller kept it simple: he would ensure the bedsit was clean and neat in time for the tours. Then, after Ben left a set of prints, Miller framed and hung them – all five of Olsen's London-period paintings, arranged clockwise around the walls in chronological order. Each Saturday morning, he would make himself scarce so that there was no chance of the tour group encountering him. Soon, though, he struck upon small improvements. By tidying away, out of sight, all of his personal effects and any trappings of modernity – his phone, CD-player, the stack of CDs, the portable TV, his paperbacks, newspapers, magazines and the like – he found that the room's appearance corresponded more closely to how it might have looked in 1914. He concealed the kitchen area behind a free-standing screen he'd discovered in a bric-a-brac market and which could be folded away after each tour. Although he was never there to witness the Danes' reactions, or their guide's, and while Ben didn't once contact him to remark upon the changes, Miller was confident that the whole 'Olsen experience' was so much more authentic, or at least less inauthentic, for the hanging of the pictures and the erasure of the bedsit's resemblance to a contemporary bachelor pad.

The furniture still troubled him, however. The wardrobe, chest of drawers and bedside table were self-assembly MDF beneath fake pine veneer that was chipped and coming unglued in places; the small dining table and its two mismatched chairs were similarly cheap and contemporary. The bed, at least, was iron-framed – and his duvet, complete with stripy IKEA cover, was soon replaced by a sheet, blanket and plain cotton counterpane. The walls, too, were okay – once white, now jaundiced with age. But, the furniture. Here, Miller's programme of improvements became more radical. Unable to hide the pieces and with nowhere to store them, he saw no option but to get rid of them altogether. They dismantled simply enough. He dumped them at night, bit by bit, in a skip outside a house refurbishment at the end of the street. The furniture was Mr Kaursar's, but so what? He could deduct it from the deposit.

From then on, Miller ate off his lap, sitting on the bed, or standing up at the kitchen counter. As for his clothes, he piled them in the fitted cupboard that housed the electric meter, vacuum cleaner and ironing board. By now the bedsit was not only less modern-looking, it was more spacious – both for him to live in, and for the Danes to visit. And, with the furniture gone, it was much easier for him to strip out the carpet and underlay and return the flooring to bare boards – the originals, by the looks – laid with a couple of old rag-rugs he'd picked up at a charity shop. Next, he swapped the curtains for a pair that were less IKEA, more William Morris.

It was about this time that Miller had the idea of installing an easel.

Once the easel was in place, it made sense to set up a canvas. And the canvas – naked as a blank page and creamy-bright in the spill of light from the window – just demanded to be painted.

Miller knew nothing of painting, beyond the art-lesson daubs of his school days. So, before daring to work on the canvas in his room, he signed up for a course. The first evening, he took along one of the Olsens (his last, *Transcendence*, 1914, oil on canvas 60 x 46 ins: Olsenmuseet, Århus, private bequest) and asked to be taught to paint like that. The tutor – a balding fiftysomething Scot in twentysomething clothes, who had never heard of Olsen – said: Paint how ye like, pal. I'm just here to gawp over yer shoulder and tell ye why it's shite. The classes turned out to be good – free materials, freedom to choose your own style and subject – and the tutor, for all his affected cynicism, knew what he was about. By the end of the ten weeks, Miller had mastered some of the basics – enough to put roughly the right colours in roughly the right places for his version of the picture to resemble Olsen's, if you didn't stand too close or look for too long. As much as anything, he had wanted to learn how to pose as a painter. How to stand, how to wield the brush, how to depict the manner, expressions and posture of an artist at work. An artist in the final slough of suicidal despond.

'He killed himself after this,' Miller said.

The art tutor gazed at the print. 'Aye, I'm no fuckin' surprised.'

Transcendence, although clearly an Olsen, was markedly unlike his previous paintings, even the others from his London period. None of these was figurative, but in their near-abstraction they did reveal discernible images – the crouched, bestial form in *Self-Portrait as an Animal*; the grimacing face in *Disaffection in Blue and Red*; the silhouetted figure in *Yellow Dawn, with Man at Window*. Even *The Roof*, his penultimate work, was scored with the lines and angles of an urban skyline viewed from a rooftop. (The rooftop three storeys above Miller's bedsit, he supposed.)

If *Transcendence* was 'of' anything, its subject was devoid of literal or near-literal representation. Just so much kaleidoscopic shape and colour arranged in rectangles. *Jackson Pollock meets Rothko*, as Miller's agent might've said. The upper part was thickly etched in brash dagger-strokes in the virulent primary colours that characterised much of Olsen's work, ruptured here and there with shards of pure black... this yielding to, or merging with, calm whites and softened swatches of secondaries – translucent greens and violets, a peachy orange blush – in the middle portion... then, shockingly, a perfect slab of jet black entirely blocking off the bottom third of the picture. Except that, on close inspection, you could detect the thinnest pinstripe of blood-red separating the middle and lower sections, its shade repeated, barely visible, in a single frosted smudge – like a thumbprint, or the faint remains of a wax seal – right at the base edge of the black. This last detail was almost impossible to spot on the print; but Miller suspected that even on the original the red mark would have been as elusive as a ghost to the inattentive viewer.

*

At the first performance, Miller was more apprehensive than he'd expected to be: the brush unsteady in his grip, the gathered Danes beyond the easel distracting him. He'd braced himself for ridicule, sure that they would break into laughter when they came in to see him there, dressed as Olsen might've been in 1914. They hadn't laughed, but his fear of their mockery lingered all the same. The clothes didn't help. Supplied by a theatrical costumier, they fitted well enough – but he was unused to them and this heightened his self-consciousness. Perhaps he should have let Ben in on his plan. All these weeks, while Miller attended the classes, the guide had brought his parties each Saturday to an unoccupied, Olsen-esque room – a lifeless tableau, its focal point the easel.

Miller had wanted his debut to be a surprise for group and guide alike. Now, in the grip of stage-fright, it was as if he had sprung this not on them but on himself. The Danes were inscrutable in their reaction to his presence, while Ben – after a flicker of initial curiosity – delivered his spiel with composure, even ad-libbing references to Miller's 'show', like it was a regular feature of the tour. But what made him most nervous was the idea of applying his first brushstroke to that canvas. During the course, the painting had felt like his own work; or, at least, like a private exercise in imitation. Here, in public, it suddenly struck him as an act of trespass. Of violation.

After what seemed an age – an intentional dramatic pause, as it must've appeared – Miller finally managed to make that first mark. Then another. And another. With each smear of paint his hand shook less, the audience blurred into the background. He knew he would get through this. At the end, there was a pattering of applause (whether for Ben or himself, he couldn't tell). Then, on their way out, the Danes filed past the canvas to see what Miller had painted, and some of them clinked coins into the wooden box that held his oils.

★

'Is that new?' Miller said.

Ben fingered the tiny disk in his cheek. It resembled a press-stud. 'Found it last week,' he said. His head, he explained, was a work-in-progress, a living sculpture of 'found objects' – bits of metal he'd picked up in the street. Miller looked closer, and saw that one of the earrings was a soda ring-pull, the protrusion from his lower lip the blunt end of a cross-headed screw. The latest piercing was indeed a press-stud.

The guide had left with his group, without a word to Miller, only to return a few minutes later as Miller was changing back into his regular clothes. He had gone directly over to the easel. Standing quietly before the partially completed painting for so long that Miller had asked about the cheek-stud simply to fill the silence.

Now, another hush. Still studying the canvas, Ben said: 'That face thing.'

'What face thing?'

'All that... *grimacing*.' The younger man gurned at him. 'What was that all about?' Then, flapping a hand in foppish agitation: 'And *this*.'

'*That* was baleful angst,' Miller said, tucking his shirt in, trying not to sound petulant. 'That was an artist at work, in the throes of relentless pessimism.'

They kept coming, the Danes. As autumn turned to winter the numbers had started to tail off, in retreat with the tourist season itself. Then the performances began – his live one-man shows, as Miller regarded them – and, gradually, the group sizes edged back up. In January and February, when London Art Tours Ltd. had planned on suspending activity until spring, there were never fewer than ten in a party, sometimes eighteen or twenty. Even with the furniture gone, it was a job to fit them all in; often Miller had to paint 'in the round', with a Dane or two peering over his shoulder. By early March, he was staging two shows each weekend to cope with demand. With the tips they dropped into his box and the cut of the takings that he'd negotiated with Ben, Miller earned almost as much playing Olsen as he did from his shifts at the call centre.

What concerned him most, however, wasn't the money, but the act. Ben's snipe at that opening matinee – the grimacing semaphore show – had got to Miller. Wounded pride mutating into self-doubt. By the following Saturday he could barely perform at all for the alarm bell of melodrama tolling in his mind with each facial expression, each gesticulation. But he worked at it. And, over the weeks, he evolved a representation of Olsen that was subtler, more restrained. For Miller, this transition led to the slow acceptance that, by concentrating on painting rather than the act of impersonation, he brought a sharper edge to the role. He had to *be* a painter, not an actor *playing* a painter. As such, his 'acting' became internalised, not externalised – it was an exercise in non-performance. Far from diffusing the poignancy, the emotional intensity of an artist labouring over his final picture – duelling with the demons of his looming suicide – this understated approach electrified his audiences. Week after week, a number of them left in tears. Miller saw that if you gave people a more or less blank screen on which to project their own interpretations, they would do. He realised, too, that he had learned more about acting in his months as Olsen than he'd done at drama school or in the years of intermittent television and theatre work.

As Ben phrased it, 'You're, like, not bad, yeah?'

Not bad at painting, either. At painting *Transcendence*, that is. Each one took six shows, and he'd begun practising in the week so that, on Saturdays, he could paint from memory and with confidence. It was like learning lines: if you didn't nail them you were prone to falter, or to *recitation* rather than *delivery*. Painting as Olsen, he delivered. (He'd even sold one finished canvas to a tour groupie for fifty quid.)

But Miller was no closer to Olsen, the man, or to why he'd killed himself.

The coming Saturday was March 18th – the anniversary of Olsen's death, and birth. There were to be five shows back-to-back, as well as a wreath-laying ceremony. Late on the Friday, Ben rolled up unannounced at the bedsit to go over the arrangements.

Miller was cleaning his brushes. He let the guide in and returned to the sink.

'Been painting?' Ben said, sitting himself down on the bed.

'Leave that!' At these words, the guide let go of the dust-sheet he'd been about to remove from the easel. Conscious of the harsh voice he had used, Miller adopted an apologetic note. 'It's just... I've been having a go at *The Roof*. It's not finished.'

'*The Roof*?'

'I figured, maybe the crucial painting wasn't the final one, but the one before.' Miller saw that this was lost on his visitor. 'He goes up on to the roof and paints what he sees – but suppose the painting isn't what he *sees*, but what's *inside* him? Thoughts of death. Thoughts of jumping.' As he spoke, he worked the brushes in turn beneath the tap. Now he paused, half-facing Ben. 'All along, I assumed *Transcendence* was the suicidal state-of-mind picture. But I've painted it so often and... nothing. Not a thing. So, I'm thinking: what if that's the picture he did afterwards?'

Ben gave him a look. 'After he jumped?'

'After he'd *decided* to jump.' Miller became aware of water dripping from his hands on to the floor; he wiped them on his tunic. 'What if *Transcendence* was the peace that came with the decision – the transition from self-loathing to tranquility to nothingness? Just black, sealed with a hint of blood so faint it's barely visible. And, then – if that's *Transcendence* – it must've been *The Roof* that...' Miller exhaled. Shrugged. 'I don't know. What do I know? Anyway, I thought I'd paint it for myself.'

'What you're doing is imposing a narrative, like, on a non-narrative form.'

'Says the art history student. Says the art history student, quoting his lecturer.'

'Yeah, whatever.' Ben had stretched out on Miller's bed, arms behind his head and feet on the pillow. 'The self is the one refuge from a hostile world.'

'What?'

'Expressionism, yeah? The only place the artist can go is inside himself. It's all me, me, me.' From his tone, he neither approved nor disapproved but was simply offering a definition. 'And when you make a story out of it, it's all you, you, you.'

Miller considered this, unpersuaded. Olsen completed those last two pictures, then killed himself. That was the story: Olsen's, not Miller's. And it must be in there, somewhere, in those strokes of paint. Before he could say this, Ben switched topics. The tour guide had slipped his feet beneath the pillow and was raising and lowering it, as though lifting weights. 'So, anyway,' he said, 'how come you're in costume?'

Miller hesitated. 'I always wear it when I'm painting.'

This was true. What he failed to mention was that, just lately, he'd taken to dressing as Olsen all the time, except when he went out. It helped him get into character quicker, more fully, than spending Saturday mornings in costume and the rest of the week in regular clothes, being himself. Miller wasn't sure why he felt uneasy about admitting this – especially to Ben, whose own head was a permanent work of art.

'Did you know Olsen was gay?' Ben said.

'You just made that up.'

'I did, actually.' The guide grinned at Miller from the bed. 'Wishful thinking.'

The sex was as athletic as Miller had imagined.

★

First thing on Saturday, Miller got the steps from his bathroom and hauled them up to the top of the building. They smelled of metal and the plastic they'd been wrapped in. Out on the fire-escape, he snapped the steps open and set them against the wall.

The rooftop was flat and featureless, apart from an elaborate television mast and a low, raised oblong that must once have been the trap-door he'd seen, blocked in, from below. It was blustery, the wind flapping at his loose-fitting costume. As he stepped off the ladder a flock of pigeons took wing, startling him, so many figure 3s sketched on the chalky morning sky. Space enough on the roof for two tennis courts, laid side by side. Even up here, there was litter: sweet and snack wrappers, a carrier bag snagged on the TV aerial like a flag at half-mast. Bird shit. Here and there, strips of roofing-felt starting to peel. A circle might have drawn him naturally to its centre, but this rectangular expanse suggested no direction and Miller found himself stalled, aimless. He supposed he might inspect the views to identify the perspective from which Olsen had made his picture. But this would surely be pointless, some one hundred years on. In any case, the urban skyline in *The Roof* was fragmentary, dislocated, so melted into a formless primary wash of colour that to 'locate' it, even back in 1914, would have been like trying to recognise a woman's face from one of Picasso's Cubist portraits. For all Miller knew, the view in Olsen's painting was a composite of several aspects, or altogether imaginary.

He hadn't come up here for that, for authentication.

Even so, he patrolled the perimeter to gaze out over London. In a high place, your eye is drawn towards the horizon. Then it is drawn to the ground, far below, where – it occurs to you, it *must* occur to you – you'd be dashed to death in however many seconds it took to fall. If you stare down long enough, hard enough, the ground gives the illusion of rushing up to meet you. *The exhilarating dread of vertigo.* This was just a phrase that formed in Miller's thoughts as he stood there, on Olsen's roof, but the sensation was genuine. He wondered if the same appalling thrill had coursed through the man himself, all that time ago. That was one thing. But how would it be to jump? Actually, to jump. To *want* to jump.

By the time the first of the day's tour parties appeared in the street below, Miller was sitting on the parapet, feet dangling over the edge.

He had been on the roof for hours. Much of the time, he'd simply lain on his back staring at the sky, at the shifting of the clouds. It occurred to him, at one point, to fetch the easel and canvas and continue working on *The Roof*. But he dismissed the idea. The wind would've made it impractical. So he had carried on with the picture in his mind, rehearsing the strokes still to be made. Trying all the while to match his thoughts to those that Olsen might've had while painting the original. This task, too, proved to be as absurd, as frustrating, as wind-blown as if Miller had actually brought his gear up on to the roof. In the end, he had assumed his position on the parapet – uncertain of the time (in costume, he wore no watch) or how long he'd have to wait, but prepared to sit there for as long as it took.

Now, there they were. Fifteen, possibly twenty. Miller picked out Ben among them. They were gathered where the wreath-laying ceremony was due to be held later on. The place where it had been decided that, for the purposes of commemoration, Olsen had landed. Directly beneath where Miller sat, gazing down.

One of the women was the first to spot him. He saw her glance up, then pause, then point. She may have said something, or made an exclamation, Miller couldn't be sure, but a sound reached him before being snatched away like a scrap of paper by the breeze. Other heads turned his way and, then, everyone was staring up at the roof.

A definite shout, this time. Ben, perhaps. The words were inaudible.

Miller chose that moment to stand up, right there on the parapet.

This coincided with a stir, a ripple, among the people below, and more sounds reached him; there was a dispersal – not that they scattered, or even parted, just that small spaces opened up where, before, they'd been closely huddled. They were more animated, too. Their gestures – the raised hands, the puppet-like arm movements, the opening and closing of mouths – appeared co-ordinated, as though he was watching a mime troupe enact a scene from a piece of experimental theatre. In that instant it struck him that what *they* saw was Olsen, on that ledge high above; the Danes were preparing for him to jump, to plummet right down upon them.

Miller smiled. Naturally that was what they'd believe they were seeing. What they failed to see, as he could – what he was unable to tell them, for the wind thieving his words – was that the roof shows you only how to die, not why.

So he waved, to let them know he was well. That he was not Olsen.

Waiting at the Pumpkin

SHE COULD HEAR DUNCAN from across the café.

'No, Malcolm... No, not an option.'

The phone was black and slim and looked, to Louisa, as if it would snap as easily as a slice of Ryvita. She approached, carrying their coffees, visualising herself reaching the table without spillage. The drinks smarted her fingers through the waxy cardboard. She set them down and returned to the counter for the pastries.

... the 16.15 Northern service to Blackpool North, calling at...

The café was cramped with people and luggage. An overheated oval filled with too-small tables and too-small chairs, its name echoed by an almost pumpkin-coloured decor of creams, oranges and clarets. Picture windows ranged around the perimeter, the glazing vibrant with the comings and goings of the trains. Louisa squeezed her feet in among the bags beneath their table. The surface was wet. She swabbed it with a serviette. Cold tea; a stewed odour that reminded her of school dinners.

'Malc, mate, it's a defo nada.'

Duncan shut off the phone. He tore a pastry free of its wrapper. Louisa watched him eat. The sleek dark hairs on the backs of his hands were so neat they might have been combed. She hadn't noticed this before and the discovery was too intimate and slightly shocking.

'Stale,' he said.

'Mine's okay.'

'Should've gone to Costa.'

His shirt was so blue it looked virtual. He produced a pack of cigarettes and lit up, releasing smoke towards the ceiling, with its too-bright spotlights.

He offered her one, grinning. 'Go on, you know you want to.'

Louisa declined. You weren't supposed to in here. But the Chinese-looking guy at the till paid them no attention. He banged coffee grounds into a bin with three metallic raps. Adele played on a radio behind the counter, ruptured by a hiss from the milk steamer.

'You'll crack,' Duncan said. 'No willpower.' He placed the cigarettes beside the phone, laying the lighter squarely on the pack. 'Twenty quid a week, I spend on these.'

'Yeah, I reckon I used to –'

'One K forty a year. Doesn't bear thinking about.'

They ate. Louisa was hungry; she'd skipped lunch to prepare for that afternoon's meeting. Tired, too. She suppressed a yawn. Her pastry was pockmarked from where the icing had adhered in gluey clots to the cellophane. She tried not to eat with conspicuous haste, measuring out each bite between sips of scalding coffee.

Platform 2 for the 16.20 Arriva Trains West service to Holyhead…

Holyhead. For the ferry to Dublin – all of Ireland opening up to you from one train journey.

Duncan inspected his watch. 'I have to put in a call to H.O. at five, so we should get cracking.' He removed a document from his case and made space for it. 'Now then.'

Ideally she'd have received a copy in advance, he said, but there hadn't been time. So what they'd do was rattle through this one together. He tapped the form with a ballpoint pen inscribed with the logo of The Palace Hotel. Louisa found herself nodding, as if the pen operated her chin on an invisible thread. His fingernails were chewed down to the flesh.

'You know, cos the VIZ were agreed last time and the

targets are... well, they've either been attained, or they haven't.' He spread his hands. 'Consensus?'

It had been a year since her previous appraisal, and she couldn't recall what VIZ stood for. Something something zones. Visible? *Vital.* Vital Improvement Zones, that was it. Louisa leaned forward, sitting awkwardly, so that she didn't have to read upside down. Her VIZ were precisely tabulated. Sales. Technical Knowledge. Time Management. Teamwork. Output. Budget. Career Development. Personal Development. She didn't remember there being so many. The plan had been to do this on the train over to Scarborough, but they'd just missed the 16.07 and had the best part of an hour to kill.

A fruit machine chugged out winnings, snagging Louisa's attention. A schoolboy scooped up the coins and began slotting them back in.

Please do not leave your luggage unattended...

Duncan was the more resonant. Each remark, each terse analysis, punctured the air, gathering glances from the other customers. That woman, with her two squabblesome sons; that balding guy, reading the *Manchester Evening News.* Louisa was aware of mumbling her responses, as if speaking in an undertone might cause Duncan to moderate his own voice. They could be mistaken for lovers quarrelling in public: one strident, oblivious to the spectacle they created; the other, seized with self-consciousness. Duncan, as a lover, wasn't something she cared to think about.

Platform 3 for the 16.33...

'I'm looking at twelve months' work, Louisa, and I'm getting... three months' worth of progress. Four, tops.' He shrugged. 'So what I'm saying is, are we operating on different satisfaction thresholds?'

'No, it's just...' She inhaled through her nose. 'It depends how you quantify... I mean, how quantifiable these things are.'

Duncan repeated 'quantifiable' to himself, in the way that

a cat investigates a piece of food before eating it.

It was soporifically warm, despite the occasional gust of cooler air from the door. She imagined picking up the appraisal document and fanning herself. As they talked, as *he* talked, she fretted at her necklace. There was a sudden commotion at the next table: one of the boys had knocked over a drink and was being scolded. Four years old, maybe five. She resisted a compulsion to tell the mother: *Please, it was an accident*.

'Louisa. Can we?'

'Sorry, miles away.'

He took her through another VIZ, then another. She raised the coffee to her lips, trailing drips on her skirt and watching them dissolve into the dark fabric. The skirt was creased from so many hours sitting in meetings. Duncan's voice reeled her in again. He was inquiring about her Time Management skills.

'There was a half-hour last Monday,' she said. 'I think I managed that quite well.'

He didn't smile. 'You want me to add "Sense Of Humour" to the list?'

Platform 4 for the 16.38...

The what service? To Norwich. The train drew to a halt just beyond their window; lurid green-and-yellow livery. Duncan pressed his cigarette stub into the remains of his pastry. A scent of tobacco and blackcurrant. The child was crying now, the mother staring out of the window as if she might hurl herself, or her son, through the glass.

'Where were we?' He frowned at the paperwork. 'Right. Career Dev.'

He pronounced it *Korea*. A man in the queue at the counter was observing them, eavesdropping. 'Couldn't we finish this on the train?' Louisa said.

'And that would make a difference to your performance rating?'

She didn't reply.

'Look,' he checked his watch again, 'there's nothing we can't wrap up now, is there?'

Louisa's fingers were tacky. When she wiped them, wafery shreds of serviette stuck to the skin. She rubbed the paper off then sucked each finger in turn. On the radio, they were playing an old Destiny's Child track. Louisa hadn't heard that song in years. The tune, the lyrics, insinuated themselves into her thoughts.

...for the 16.41 Transpennine Express service to Liverpool Lime Street...

Duncan ignited another cigarette, eyes shuttered against the fumes.

Sheathing the document in a clear plastic wallet, he replaced it in the case and snapped the latches shut.

'Good. Job done.'

Louisa looked down at the table. She could have rested her head on her arms and fallen asleep right there, among the debris and the glistening dandruff of sugar granules.

'Wazz alert,' Duncan said. 'Did you notice where they were?'

Louisa pointed beyond the farthest window, to the twin doors obscured by a blur of bodies funnelling through the ticket barriers. Duncan went outside. She observed his progress, the opening and slow closing of the door to the Gents. His cigarettes, lighter and phone lay in neat slabs where he'd left them. She craved a cigarette. Longed to sit there, smoking his cigarettes one after another. At the next table, the boys were being readied to leave. Catching the mother's eye, Louisa smiled, but the woman's expression hardened against her.

... left unattended may be removed or destroyed by the security services...

Louisa yawned. *The objective, Louisa, is to develop a collective and individual culture of excellence.* There was to be another appraisal in four months instead of twelve. Which was fine.

Better than she'd expected – or had a right to expect, was Duncan's inference. Her gaze drifted to the platforms. It amazed her that all these trains could pass in and out of the station without collision. A fluke of integration.

She closed her eyes and took deep breaths. When she re-opened them she was staring at Duncan's cigarettes. He was right: it was a question of willpower. The power of the will.

He would return in a moment, make his call to head office, then they would head out to platform 4 in time for the Scarborough train; another night in a smart hotel, another day of meetings to come. By Wednesday, they'd be back at their desks, her appraisal to be printed off, in triplicate, and filed. She would receive her copy. Louisa went to massage her eyes but stopped herself, on account of the make-up.

The door to the Gents remained shut.

There were rumours, at work, that Duncan would take himself off to the toilets now and then to do a line. Louisa was unconvinced. He didn't seem the type, if there *was* a type. Another rumour was that he'd been overheard in one of the cubicles, sobbing. That didn't strike her as any more credible, but it was the story she preferred to believe. What interested her was that his colleagues – Louisa herself – had the need to conceive of an alternate Duncan, a counterpoint to the version they worked with.

The train approaching platform 2 is the 16.48 Transpennine Express service to Barrow-in-Furness and Windermere...

That would be nice. Spot of hill walking, picnics, pub lunches. Lovely little guest house with a view over the water; being woken in the morning by the bleating of sheep.

The thought must've occurred first, but the deed was so unhesitating as to seem simultaneous. A reflex. Reaching across the table, she picked up Duncan's phone – even lighter and less substantial that she'd anticipated – and slipped it into his unfinished coffee, causing the cup to overflow. Only the tip of the phone, a shiny-black corner, was visible at the surface, like a shark's fin in miniature.

There. Easy as that.

She would've expected her hands to be tremulous. But they were perfectly steady. Louisa stood up, gathered her bags and, without glancing in the direction of the door to the toilets, left the café and set off across the footbridge to platform 2, her heels ticking on the steps. She'd need a pair of boots, socks, the right clothes. A mini-rucksack, an O/S map. Tomorrow morning: a lie in, a proper B&B breakfast, kit herself out at one of those outdoor pursuits shops, then a brisk hike along the lake shore.

Louisa visualised herself doing all of that.

The Windermere train pulled in as she descended towards the platform. A momentary panic quickened her pace. But she saw there was no need to rush: passengers were disembarking, others waiting to board. There would be time for her to make it before the doors closed.

The Sayer of the Sooth

LOGAN STANDS AT THE basin in the en suite bathroom and raises his eyes to his reflection. All day, he stares at faces. Studies the data that leak from them. Compiles the analyses. Composes his reports. But those are other's faces. His own, he can hardly bear to look at anymore. Tonight, though, he makes himself linger before the lightly tinted glass, holding the gaze that holds his.

On one of the early dates with Mia he stood at the mirror in a pub restroom and looked himself in the face, just as he is doing now.

'Why would she be interested in *you*, you sad, old, ugly bastard?' he said out loud.

He was 44, she was 31. He's 56 now. They've been together the same length of time that his first marriage lasted. Which goes to show. Logan doesn't know what it goes to show, exactly. He doesn't know anything these days. Those features in the mirror belong to a stranger.

Through the closed door, he hears Mia in the bedroom. A drawer opens, the dressing-table stool creaks. She'll be stripping away her day-face and applying her night-face. He pictures her: the raised eyebrows, the widened eyes, the flared nostrils, the elongated O of her mouth as she stretches the skin across the bones of her skull. Her dark hair, scraped into a ponytail.

In his head, Logan rehearses the conversation they'll have when he leaves the bathroom. The trick will be to slip the key question in as if it carries no more weight than anything else.

How was Kirsten?

He has to make sure they're looking directly at one another when he asks it.

Logan removes a small case and a bottle of fluid from his dressing-gown pocket and places them on the ledge of the basin. He draws the dropper from the bottle. Tilts his head back and squeezes a couple of drips into his left eye, then two more into his right.

Mia is humming. He can't make out the tune through the bathroom door.

How was Kirsten?

There's a metallic taste in his mouth. His fingers tremble as he stows the bottle back in his pocket. Logan composes himself. Once his hands are steady again, he clicks open the case and lifts out the first of the lenses on the tip of his little finger.

Thats how the story begins.

My greatgrandfather wrote it far back in 2014 – 35 years before I was born – and here it is in a science fiction anthology. Granny Josephine sent it me.

A literal paper book in the literal mail. Hugely old and creased and yellowy.

The note tucked inside said 'Jack, I came across this when I was sorting out some boxes of my dad's stuff and thought you might be interested. The stories are all set in 2070! I don't recall ever reading his, however I do vaguely remember him promising to make me and your Great-Aunt Polly characters in it. As you'll see, he didn't. Granny J xx'

I never knew greatgrandad (long passed by the time I turned up) although I have read one of his novels – Granny J gifted it me when I started e-uni. Didnt rate it. But then I dont like any of the late Second Elizabethans. To be honest if it hadnt been for the 2070 coincidence I doubt Id have bothered to read this short story.

Youd never know it was set in 2070 from the opening scene though.

Maybe he couldnt imagine what a bathroom would be like 56 years into the future so decided to play safe and keep it neutral. Im guessing the lenses are mind reading devices. And its obvious the woman – Mia (is that a name?) – has told Logan she was out with this friend Kirsten when shes actually been cheating on him.

Ha! Just tried to use voice-activation to turn the page! Glad Dex wasnt here to see me do *that*.

Looks like we leave the bathroom scene now to fill in some backstory. Yawnsome.

Logan had worked at TruTell for nine years before applying to transfer to the NPD section. Not that he was authorised to know which new products were in development at that stage. First there was the interview, psychometrics, induction. Only once he'd passed and had thumbed a confidentiality agreement

He thinks we use *thumbprints* to sign documents in 2070?!

was he granted access to the part of the complex known as 'the bunker'. Mia had no idea. He couldn't tell anyone outside the company the true nature of his job. He explained away the salary increase and longer hours as the result of a promotion within the data-rationalising section.

The paradox of lying about a job in the lie-detection business wasn't lost on Logan.

Skimming down the text I see it goes on like this for another half page or so: Whole place is buzzing with rumours about the latest R&D... after so long working on TruTells traditional progs and apps Logans excited to be at the cutting edge... Blardyblardyblardy.

Im already getting eye strain from reading on-paper. And all that *punctuation*.

Out of curiosity I search TruTell (on Mi-fi after tapping the word on the page a couple of times before I figured out why nothing was happening). No such company. Pity. It wouldve been good and spooky if the old boy had invented a business that had literally come into existence. Not that greatgrandad was all that old when he wrote this. 54. Two years younger than Logan. He didnt even have the imagination to create a lead who wasnt his own gender and roughly the same age.

Its too easy to see where the lie detection angle is headed when we eventually get Logan from the bathroom to the bedroom. The cheating wife. The questions he plans to ask her while he's wearing those hitech lenses.

I could write the rest of the story myself.

> Logan settled into a seat across the desk from the project manager. Jaswinder Kaur. *Please call me Jazz.* Late 30s. Bright-eyed, intelligent-looking. Her bare forearms ought to have been hirsute but were smooth and hairless. Only the lower half of her face smiled.
>
> 'Welcome to the bunker, Jack.'

Hey Logan has the same first name as me! Good one greatgrandad.

As they talk Im not picturing Jazz too well. Which gives me an idea.

'Mi-screen' I say and the wall across the room blooms into light. Dont know why I didnt think of it before. I hold up the book at the scene Im reading. 'Scan text and play.'

2D or 3D? Mi-screen asks.

'2D.' Dex thinks Im weird but I cant be doing with immersive. Makes me queasy.

The wallcam gives a single bright-white blink and there they are – Jaswinder Kaur and Jack Logan – chatting across a desk. The avatars are defaults. Her voice is too cheerful but at least she has dark hair and skin. As for Logan he looks like that guy who massacred all those people last month at the climate refugee camp.

I v/a the story to pause while I customise them. Hugely better.

'Resume.'

Shes briefing Logan about the project and Im tempted to overnarrate and have them fuck right there on the desk. I don't though. This is my greatgrandads story after all.

She placed a small transparent case and a bottle of eye-drops on the desk in front of him.

'Contact lenses?' Logan asked.

'Go on, try them.' Jazz Kaur smirked, like a conjuror about to name the mystery playing card a member of the audience had picked from a deck.

Once the lenses were in, he let his gaze roam: the unpatterned grey floor-covering, the spiky leaves of a yucca, the reflection of a ceiling light-panel on the desk's glossy surface. Finally, Jazz's face. Everything looked exactly as it had before.

'Ask me a question,' she said. 'Anything you like.'

With so much choice, his mind went blank. He shrugged. 'Why am I wearing them?'

'Because I want you to see for yourself what the prototype does.' As she finished speaking, Logan could have sworn there was a brief flash of green light before his eyes. 'Ask me something else,' she said. 'Ask me my name.'

'Okay, what's your name?'

'My name is Jack Logan,' the woman said.

This time the flash was red. Logan laughed.

'I know.' Jazz was smiling with the whole of her face now. 'Tell me if I'm getting too technical for you, here, but in NPD this is what we call fucking incredible.'

A flash of amber this time.

Pointing to his eyes, Logan said, 'So, this is—'

'Silent Talker in a pair of contact lenses. Yes, that's exactly what it is.' *Green light.*

'But the colours—'

'Visible only to the wearer. Same as with the glasses.' *Green.*

'There have been Silent Talker *glasses*?'

'Yes. But you're not authorised to know that.' *Green.* 'I'm afraid I'll have to kill you now, Jack.' *Red.*

Logan laughed again. He took out both lenses and held one of them between thumb and middle finger, studying it, raising it to the light. 'The software?' he asked. 'Camera, mic?'

'Integrated into the lenses,' Jazz said. 'The size of the transistors wasn't too much of an issue. It was quite some job, though, to produce conductive paths narrow enough to connect it all up but wide enough to carry an electron. And to make everything transparent, of course.'

'Of course.'

She must have picked up on Logan's tone. 'Oh, same here – I'm just quoting what the guys and gals in Materials told me.'

'What about power?' Logan asked. 'I mean, are we talking about... what, an invisible battery tiny enough to fit into a contact lens? And with enough capacity to actually work?'

'Who was it who said that any advanced technology is indistinguishable from magic?'

'Arthur C. Clarke. And it was '*sufficiently* advanced'.'

'Sufficiently. Yes.' Jazz indicated the lens Logan was holding. 'The battery converts energy from blinking and eye-movement into electricity to maintain the charge while you're wearing them. The lenses are *powered by your eyes* – isn't that some way north of phenomenal?'

'Don't they heat up, though?'

'What do I have to do to impress you?'

'You could tell me they won't burn holes in people's eyes,' Logan said.

'Look, I can't even pronounce the stuff these lenses are made of but, with the eye-drops, they test to 60-minute pre-discomfort endurance. No corneal damage. No allergenic issues. No holes. Gesturing for him to pass her the lenses, she said, 'Here, let me show you the upload.'

Jazz produced a thicker than usual mem-stick from a drawer and pressed each lens into an aperture in its side, then inserted the stick in a port in the drive panel on her desk. On the screen along one side of her work station, the plain grey floor pulled into focus, then the yucca plant, and so on, until the picture settled on the project manager's face. Her voice rang out sharp and clear. *Ask me a question. Anything you like.*

The glasses I mightve believed. But lie detection contact lenses with invisible miniaturised components? From a writer who cant even imagine the details of a 2070 bathroom. What next: Logan flies home from work in his jetpack to be greeted at the door by the automated yapping of a pet robo-dog?

Indistinguishable from magic. Thats an easy out for an SF writer isnt it?

I pause the story. 'Search for Silent Talker' I say.

A block of text appears in front of Jazzs freezed face. Yawnsome. I v/a audio.

Silent Talker was a computerised, non-invasive psychological profiling system for the collection and analysis of non-verbal behaviour. By means of Artificial Neural Networks, the system used multiple channels of micro-observations of a filmed subject to determine his or her psychological state when speaking. Its primary application was the detection of, and distinguishing between, truthful and deceptive non-verbal signal patterns.

'Simplify for fucks sake.'

For fuck's sake' is an exclamation which indicates—

'No. Simplify Silent Tal—'

It hits me that Mi-fi *deliberately* misunderstood me. This is Dexs doing — overwriting the program to enable Randomised Disambiguation Failure. It passes for humour in the IT realm she inhabits. I fall for it every time.

'Very funny' I say.

Is it my imagination or does Mi-fi sound just a little pleased with itself as it gives me the proper answer?

Silent Talker used computer analysis of faces to tell whether people were lying.

'More. History.'

Silent Talker was invented and patented in the first decade of the 21st Century by a team of computing scientists at Manchester Metropolitan University. After successful trials and further refinements, yielding an accuracy rate of >90%, Silent Talker attracted interest from investors. Rebranded as F.A.C.E. (Facial Analysis and Classification Evaluator) — or the 'lying eye', as it became popularly known — the system entered commercial production in 2020 and by the end of that decade was in widespread use in the UK — for example, among police, security, intelligence and border control agencies, as well as in legal proceedings and in the prevention of welfare fraud. Other markets soon opened up and by the 2040s F.A.C.E. had established itself as the leading international brand in anti-deception technology (ADT).

Oh well everyones heard of the lying eye. Never mind writing a short story about it – greatgrandad shouldve bought shares.

'More history' I say. 'Anything on lie detection glasses or contact lenses?'

F.A.C.E. Inc. launched a glasses version in 2055 but the prohibitive cost and media 'scare' stories about the risk of eye damage and brain tumours resulted in poor sales and the product was discontinued in 2058. No historical information on ADT contact lenses.

So. Poor old Jack Logan – a cheating wife a dud plot and a pair of hitech lenses that are approximately 100% fairy dust. I should put the book down. But with Dex at her job interview and no virtual lectures today Ive nothing better to do.

'TruLens is the holy grail,' Jazz told Logan. 'Non-detectable lie-detection.'

He waited for her to continue.

'Using Silent Talker on traditional devices – cameras, cams, phones, droids and so on – there's little or no chance to hide the fact that the viewee is being filmed,' she said. 'Even with TruSpecs, the problem was –'

'Their high cost and the fear of blindness and brain cancer' I say.

'– that, once their existence was public knowledge, no matter how carefully we designed them to look like regular glasses, they ran the risk of viewees suspecting they were being lie-detected.'

'Not to mention the cost. Or the fear of blindness and brain cancer.'

Logan nodded. 'And if the view*er* didn't usually wear glasses—'

'Exactly. With TruLens, though... imagine it, Jack – one day, anyone who can afford a pair of the little cuties will never be deceived again.'

'But, surely,' Logan said, 'if TruLens becomes popular then there's *always* the possibility of being lie-detected. In every conversation, by everyone we meet. And if other people can wear them without us ever being sure of it, the whole world is going to be clamouring for a pair.'

Jazz grinned. 'Do you want to break the bad news to Sales and Marketing?'

Logan loved working on TruLens.

In those early months, the prototype was trialled in-house, with members of the team as viewer and viewee. His task was to analyze the footage and compile his reports. Any hardware or software glitches would be fixed ahead of the lenses being tested 'out there', as Jazz called the world beyond the perimeter fence of TruTell HQ.

After the cancellation of TruSpecs, this new project – this *holy grail* – electrified the team in the bunker and Logan couldn't help being caught up in it all. For a time, at least.

'Logans avatar.' And there he is gazing out at me from the wall-screen.

Hes dressed in smart-casual office clothes from the early 2060s to show hes out of date compared to his younger colleagues. Ive made him look like greatgrandad I realise – what Ive seen of him in old photos. Tall thinning on top and round shouldered. Ive given him (Logan) the big nose that he (greatgrandad) gave dad and me.

'Edit expression. Edit posture. Logan dislikes himself. Logan thinks hes unattractive and old. Logan suspects his wife of cheating on him. Logans afraid of losing her.'

As I speak the avatar reconfigures. He looks like a man impersonating a dog that thinks its about to be whacked with a stick for pooping on the carpet.

Forget about the plot and the technology – Logans the point here Ive realised.

What happened between him starting in NPD full of excitement at working on TruLens and the scene in the bathroom? The man who can hardly bear to look at himself in the mirror. Who doesnt know anything anymore. Whos sure his wife is screwing around.

Text message from Dex Comms says.

'Convert to audio.'

Lo Jacko. Presentation ok-ish. Interview in 10m. Eeek! XX

Audio always turns her into a 5 year old with a cold. As for the kisses they sound like something off Pornflix. The *eeek* surprises me. Dex didnt seem hugely nervous this morning considering. 'I wont get the job is why' she said.

'Go lady!' I say. 'Send.'

Reply from Dex: You doing?

'Reading.'

Hahahaha

I send an X and shut off Comms.

Logans still there on the wall. I undo the edit to make him look how he did before, then scan and play the next couple of pages.

He opened the next file. A young man appeared, visible from the chest up, freeze-framed. Logan stared at the screen, hunched at a desk as though his head was too heavy for him to hold upright. When he finally spoke, his voice sounded flat, dull.

'TL-0127. Caucasian male, 25–30; interior of train compartment. Blond fringe covers most of forehead but sufficient observable channels in rest of face. Average profile exposure, 91.55% full frontal. Distance, viewer to viewee, 124cm. Both seated. Viewer I.D.: NPD 03TL – McCormack, R. Time and date of contact: 13.27 – 09/24/2070. Duration of contact, 8m 40s.'

Logan raised both hands to his face and rubbed his eyes. Eventually, he lowered them again. Refocused on the screen.

He pressed play.

It was evident that the NPD undercover operative and the viewee were unknown to one another and that McCormack had initiated the conversation by commenting on the weather. As they talked, Logan recorded his observations, pausing the film at each flash of red, amber or green. These responses, Logan replayed, logged, time-coded and classified.

In eight minutes and forty seconds, the blond man lied seventeen times. He lied about:

his shoes letting in water;

an online documentary he claimed to have seen;

the end-point of his journey;

the nature of his job;

his attitude towards migrant workers;

not having a pen the viewer could borrow...

One lie after another. Logan logged them all. When the footage ended, he compiled his stats report and analysis then stored them in the TruLens cache along with the film itself.

After a moment, he called up the next file. Opened it. Closed it. Opened it. Closed it.

'That function seems to be operating normally,' a voice behind him said.

Logan started, swivelled round in his seat. 'Hey, Jazz. Sorry, I didn't —'

'You must be due a break, aren't you?' Then, without waiting for him to reply, 'Me too. Let's grab a drink and a couple of slices of fresh air.'

In the octagonal garden behind 'the bunker', Jaswinder Kaur set her juice down on a picnic table but remained standing. Her black hair had a bluey sheen in the daylight. Logan stood beside her, drink in hand. They gazed at the fountain, its loud splashes competing with the traffic's relentless electric whine on the freeway beyond the perimeter fence. Droplets of water had settled like dew on the vibrantly green synthetic lawn.

'You seem unhappy, Jack.'

'Me?' He sipped his drink. 'Long morning, that's all.'

'Not just today. This week. Last week.'

Logan didn't respond.

'A hundred files so far,' Jazz said. 'That's a lot of reports.'

'A hundred and twenty-seven.' The breeze strengthened and a fine mist from the fountain settled on Logan's skin. He shuddered. 'It's not the workload, it's the —'

'Work itself. I know.'

They stood in silence for a moment.

'Before I switched to NPD I didn't think anything of it,' Logan said. 'The lying. Crime suspects, benefits claimants, asylum seekers. It goes with—'

'The territory. Yes.'

He gave a dry laugh. 'We used to call them the Red-Light Districts.'

'You didn't expect it from ordinary people in everyday contexts?' Jazz nodded as if in response to her own question. 'People with no apparent reason to lie or anything to gain by it.'

'Not so much of it, no. But the red–amber–green ratios on this project are more or less the same as they've been on all the others.'

'We are a species of liars, Jack.'

He turned to look at her. 'You sound very matter-of-fact about it.'

'Yesterday,' she said, returning his gaze with that half-smiling face, 'my son showed me a picture he'd done at school. It was awful, even for a six-year-old. I told him it was really good.'

'That's different.'

'Okay, what about when I say you don't seem happy and you tell me it's just been a long morning. If I'd been wearing lenses, would that have scored a green light. Or a red?'

He took a moment to reply. 'I know we all lie. I know it's part of *the rich, complex fabric of human interaction and social cohesion* – Christ, you had me jump through enough psychometric hoops to get this job.' Logan shook his head. 'It's just that–'

'You don't like witnessing hundreds of lies a day every day by people just like you.'

'Thanks for finishing another of my sentences for me, Jazz.'

The project manager laughed. 'Sorry, I do that, don't I?' Then, serious again, 'But the thing is – if you hate the smell of shit, don't become a pig farmer.'

'Overnarrate: Logan says *Fuck you*.'

On the wall Logans avatar turns to Jazzs avatar and says 'Fuck you.'

Back at his work station, he opened the next file in the queue. It was another from McCormack. This time she

was at home, in the kitchen, talking to her boyfriend
  Logan closed it and opened a different one instead.

'Pause.'

I wonder if he was already suspicious of Mia at this point.
Or maybe hed *always* suspected he would lose her one day. It
was just a question of when and who to. Right from that early
date when he saw his ugly old reflection in a restroom and
prepared himself for rejection. Okay so shed stuck with him all
this time. Proved him wrong. But if you have a set of scales
with a 12 year relationship on one side and a lifetime of
insecurities on the other – which weighs the most?

What do I know? Dex and me havent been together 12
months.

Theyre fictional characters. I realise that. Theres no Mia.
No Jack Logan. But I really hope when he steps out into that
bedroom and asks 'How was Kirsten?' Mia will say 'Yeah fine
she was in good form – it was lovely to see her' or something
like that... and Logans lenses will flash green.

'Resume.'

But the scene only plays for a few seconds more before
reaching the end of the part Id scanned. I pick up the book
again and skim down the next page.

Greatgrandad obviously wanted to make sure the reader
understood just how hugely Logans job was messing with his
head. As the weeks go by and he watches the lies pile up his
mood sinks lower... barely talks to the rest of the team...
outside work he distrusts everyone he meets... cant stand to
look people in the face... irritable... sleeping badly... drinking
too much... Blardyblardy.

Oh here this is more like it. Hes at home with Mia.

Logan pretended not to notice Mia's look as he pulled
a bottle of red from the rack, unscrewed the cap and
filled most of a glass.

'You sure?' he asked gesturing at the bottle.

'No. I'm good, thanks.' Her smile resembled Jaswinder Kaur's.

I pause to adjust Mia. For one thing she has a blonde bob even though she was described at the start of the story as having dark hair long enough for a ponytail. But I didnt scan that scene so how could Mi-screen know? I change the blue dress for a plain yellow short sleeve top and white cords and give her a wrist tattoo (like Dexs) in the style of a plaited rainbow.

I make her less pretty. If shes not so attractive maybe shell be less likely to cheat on Logan. It doesn't work like that I know but its the least I can do for him.

'Smells interesting,' Logan said.

'Quinoa tabbouleh.'

'There's no need for that kind of language.'

Mia didn't laugh. Logan didn't expect her to.

She told him dinner would be ready in ten minutes. He swallowed some wine. When neither of them said anything else, he raised the glass to his lips again. He watched her fetch salad things and set them on the counter. Watched her shred lettuce into a bowl. As she sliced cucumber, pepper, tomatoes, he went on watching her. Watching her face the whole time, not her hands. All the while, sipping his drink.

Mia stopped. Placed both hands against the edge of the worktop, the knife still clasped in her fingers. She looked like she was trying to push the counter across the kitchen towards him.

Without raising her gaze from the chopping board, she said, 'Don't stare at me.'

'I'm not staring.'

'Please, Jack. Just don't.'

'I like watching you.'

'You could lay the table.' She looked up at him now. 'That would be good.'

'Right. I'll do that. I'll lay the table.'

Logan remained where he was. Took another mouthful of wine.

'Or you could just stay sober till we're the other side of dinner.'

'Which is it: lay the table or stay sober? I can't do both.'

Mia held his gaze a moment then, without speaking, went back to preparing the salad.

Jack. JackJackJack. You might as well drive her straight round to the other feller's flat.

As for people in 2070 making salad that way.

At the end of the meal, most of the food remained uneaten. Logan went to replenish his glass but the wine was done. He set the bottle back down. Mia had already begun to clear the table.

'Oh – a guy at work offered me two tickets for one of the Korsakoff recitals,' Logan said, his voice stilted with the effort required not to slur the words. 'If you fancy it.'

'When is it?'

'Friday.'

'We can't, then, can we?' Making her way to the waste-disposal, Mia said, 'That's the night I'm meeting up with Kirsten.'

'Right. Yeah, I'd forgotten about that.' His eyes trailed her across the room. 'Maybe you and Kirsten could use the tickets?'

She didn't think Korsakoff would be Kirsten's thing.

Okay so were heading into endgame. Finally. I upload the last few pages and away we go.

The next scene is like something out of a spydram. The problem is the TruLens kits will be security tagged and greatgrandad has to come up with a plausible way for Logan to smuggle one out of 'the bunker' without authorisation. A *whole page* though? Anyway we already know he gets away with it because the story began with him at home about to put the lenses in his eyes. So wheres the tension the suspense the drama?

I fastforward.

Were back in that bathroom. The narrative reverts to present tense. In goes the first lens. Then the second. Logan stands in front of the mirror staring at his reflection.

> Logan stands in front of the mirror, staring at his reflection. Steadies his breathing. From the bedroom come sounds of Mia slipping into bed.
>
> She didn't take a shower when she returned from her evening out. That proves nothing, though. She could have showered there, with him. Wherever 'there' was. Whoever 'he' might be. They didn't kiss when she came home and so Logan never got close enough to tell whether she smelled of soap, or sex, or no different to when she'd gone out.
>
> None of it matters now.
>
> The answer is the other side of that door. He only has to ask the question.

'Pause.'

What occurs to me here is that nowhere in the story has there been any evidence of Mia cheating on him. No hints or clues or suspicious behaviour. Apart from the dinner scene shes been out of shot the whole time. Their relationship too – all off camera. If we read anything into the things Mia says and does in that kitchen – her *manner* towards Logan – its only because weve been primed by his belief that shes seeing another guy.

Thats all we have to go on: Logans distrust.

So one of two things is happening – there have been plenty of hints and clues and suspicious behaviour over the weeks leading up to the bathroom scene but greatgrandad

a) forgot to tell us about them or

b) deliberately left them out.

Now okay he wasnt the greatest writer of his generation but he turned out enough novels and short stories to make me pretty sure were not talking 'a' here.

Why leave out all that stuff on purpose though?

Unless 'b' is meant to lead us to a third alternative:

c) there have been no hints clues or suspicious behaviour whatsoever.

Logan goes to the bathroom door. Rests his forehead against it, each breath coating the sleek surface with a film of condensation.

He only has to touch the panel and the door-lock will release.

'Overnarrate.'

'Logan cant go through with it' I say. 'Cant open that door cant step into that bedroom cant ask Mia that question. Cant go on being the kind of man he has become: eaten up by jealousy suspicion insecurity and paranoia – hating Mia because of an affair that exists entirely in his imagination. Hating himself for hating her.'

On the screen he remains at the door. Blinking. Breathing.

'Logan takes a step back.'

Logan takes a step back.

'He removes one of the lenses. Then the other.'

He removes one of the lenses then the other.

'He goes over to the WC.'

He goes over to the WC.

'He shakes the lenses like dice in the palm of his hand and releases them into the bowl. They barely make a sound as they hit the water.'

He shakes the lenses and releases them into the water with barely a sound.

'Logan stares down into the bowl. He activates the flush.'

On the screen his avatar does the same, gazing down into the swirl of water.

If I say 'save overnarration' my ending becomes the way the story ends. Easy as that.

Greatgrandads ending will still be right there in the book of course but I dont have to read it. I can just put it on a shelf and forget about it. I dont ever need to find out how the original version of the story ends or what happens to Logan and Mia or any of that.

Those words he wrote in 2014 belong to me now and I can do what I like with them.

And yet, and yet... I must know his ending. I can't not know it.

'Undo overnarration. Play.'

When Logan steps into the bedroom, Mia says, 'I thought you'd drowned in there.'

'Dodgy tummy,' he tells her. It's not untrue; he feels as if he might be sick right now.

Mia is sitting up in bed, browsing her slate. Flicking through messages by the look of it. In the haze from the bedside lightstick, her freshly cleansed face is unnaturally pale, her brown eyes glinting with amber. They track from left to right as she reads.

He stands at the foot of the bed, facing her.

'How was your evening?' Mia asks, without glancing up.

'I haven't had anything to drink, if that's what you're asking.'

This is a lie. But it has the intended effect of dragging Mia's attention from the screen.

'In fact,' she says, 'it wasn't what I was asking.' *Red light.*

Logan returns her stare. 'How about you?'

'Have *I* been drinking?' Is she smiling at him, or to herself? 'Yes.' *Green light.*

He thinks she's going to lower her gaze again. She doesn't. Her expression is unreadable and he almost wonders whether Mia knows about the lenses and is offering her face up to him.

This is his moment.

'I meant, how was your evening?' He keeps his voice even. 'How was Kirsten?'

Here? He ends the story *here*!?

So were supposed to figure out for ourselves whether she... I throw the book across the room and it hits the wall-screen and flaps to the floor like a dying bird.

Its my fault for being drawn in. Christ I was even starting to feel sorry for Logan.

I scrapped *my* version for *this*?

Its not just the cop-out ending its the whole fucking thing really. A *love story*. My greatgrandfather is handed an amazing piece of technology and the chance to play soothsayer – to imagine any kind of future he cares to and write whatever he likes – and he comes up with a story about a feller whose wife is (or isnt) cheating on him. Oldest most unoriginal tale in the world. He doesn't even do the SF properly. Take away the lenses and it could be 2014 2070 or any year you like since Darwin invented apes.

Call that speculative fiction? Call yourself a futurologist?

The rest of the morning Im pissed off with Greatgrandad. With myself too for letting it burrow under my skin. The story. Logan. Mia. Even after an hour of Mi-Chi I still catch myself wondering how she answered his question. Whether the lenses flashed green or red.

I take a shower to rinse off the sweat from the workout.

And as I step out the bathroom I picture Logan stepping out of his.

Im eating lunch when Comms says *Text message from Dex*.

I check the time. I was expecting her back before now. 'Convert to audio.'

Lo Jacko. Interview over. That nasal childlike voice Comms gives her.

'Howd it go?'

If badly is zero and good is 10 I reckon 4.

I send a sadface. Shell have done better than she says. Shell get the job. 'You on your way home?'

Its a moment before the next message pings.

Thing is I just bumped into an old schoolfriend on the way to the Trans stop. Havent seen her for years. So she says do I want to have lunch over this side of town and maybe take in a gallery after?

I think about this. 'Convert to visual.'

Comms says *Visual blocked by sender. Text or Audio only.*

Jacko?

'Why no vis Dex?'

Sorry. Its this stupid phone.

'Yeah?'

So anyway Ill be back this evening. Okay?

'Which old schoolfriend?'

Oh you dont know her.

'Whats her name?'

There's another delay. Then a ping and even before Dex speaks I know — I just *know* — what shes going to say.

Kirsten.

In Anticipation of the Queen

TERENCE WAS IN ANTICIPATION of the Queen. An individual roast turkey ready meal with all the trimmings was in the oven, timed to be consumed in front of the television as the broadcast began. He arranged a plate, cutlery, condiments and cracker on a tray and poured a glass of sherry. He sat in his armchair, drinking. It was sticky and tasted of apricot; he opened and closed his mouth for the curiosity of feeling the lips seal and separate. It sounded like two segments of satsuma being peeled apart.

The noise from next door started up again.

Terence set the glass down and pressed the heels of his hands against his head, just above the ears, until the quietening came. A door slammed, a shadow made a diagonal stripe across his living-room window. Terence went over to look through the net curtain and saw the woman, her back to him, standing at the kerb and apparently smoking a cigarette. It was raining and she wore a thin cotton dress, her black hair piled up on her head. She shifted her weight from one foot to the other. There was more commotion, an incoherent discharge that seemed to Terence to issue from within the adjoining wall itself, as though the neighbouring house was shouting at his. The woman turned sideways, flinching, and he saw now that she was crying, heavily pregnant and wearing slippers in the style of two fat turtles.

'D'you mind if I use your loo?'

He wouldn't have opened the door, but he knew she'd

seen him at the window. The woman wiped her face with the flat of her hand, creating a smudge beneath one eye. The cigarette was unlit. She must have noticed him staring at it.

'I can't smoke.' She stroked her belly, trying to smile. 'Thirty-nine weeks. She's using my bladder as a trampoline. I'm Monica, by the way.'

'Terence.'

When Monica returned from the bathroom, the mark beneath her eye was gone and her skin was shiny and slightly damp. An expletive entered the room from next door with perfect clarity.

'That's Judd,' she said. 'He's trying to fix the lights.'

Terence recalled passing their window the other evening: MERRY XMAS spelled out in alternating red and green, with a team of illuminated reindeer pulling Santa on a sleigh across the top of the letters. One of the deer had a red nose which flashed on and off and the window was frosted with fake snow.

'I thought the lights looked quite jolly,' he said.

'Tacky, is what they look.' Monica raised the unlit cigarette, drew on it and exhaled through her nose. It was possible to imagine two cones of smoke. 'He can't do DIY without effing and jeffing. I'm not having this one listen to that.'

'The baby?'

'They can hear in the womb, you know. A dog barked at me the other day and I felt her jump inside me, like she was scared or something.'

The couple had moved in only a few months earlier and, beyond an occasional acknowledgement in the street, Terence had exchanged no words with them. These days he exchanged few words with any of his neighbours; he was the last of his generation now that Lily next door was gone. He tried to picture Monica's husband, Judd, but all he could remember of him was short dark hair and red shoes and nothing in between.

'When it's cold,' Terence said, 'Your stress hormone levels rise and you produce more urine.' They were in the living-room doorway, staring at the blank screen of the television. He smiled. 'An alternative to your trampoline theory.'

Monica looked at him.

'Would you care for a sherry?'

'Can't drink, either.'

'How about an empty glass?'

She reciprocated his smile, covering her mouth, then the smile expanded into a laugh. 'Yeah, why not. An empty glass of sherry would be lovely.'

'On your own for Christmas, then?'

Terence nodded. 'My wife died three years ago. Violet.'

'Haven't you any family?'

'Scattered.' He mimed the geographical spread of children, grandchildren. 'I expect the phone calls will start, after the Queen.'

Monica took a moment to register the allusion. 'Judd won't have her on.'

A hammering reverberated in the dividing wall, three dull clumps accompanied by a chain of furious inarticulacy. Terence supposed that electrical repairs would be a quiet operation, not requiring the use of a hammer. He said as much to Monica. She explained that, during any DIY project, Judd would periodically remove a painting hanging in their living room, strike the wall as violently as he could with a wooden mallet, then put the picture back to conceal the damage.

'It releases his frustration,' Monica said. 'He works right at the edge, you know.'

'A safety valve?'

'Exactly.'

'Couldn't he hit the other wall – the one that doesn't have my house next to it?'

'We don't have a picture on that wall.'

Terence watched her sip from the empty glass. The unlit cigarette was poised on the rim of a saucer he'd fetched for her to use in lieu of an ashtray. He looked at the clock. She would be on in a quarter of an hour.

'Something smells good,' Monica said.

'Turkey.'

'Yeah, I've got one on the go. I'm not keen myself, but you've got to, haven't you?' She paused. 'We usually go to his folks one year and mine the next, but what with me being so close...'

Terence poured himself a second sherry. This was shaping up to be quite convivial.

'My due date is the thirtieth,' she said, 'but we're hoping to hang on for a New Year's Day baby. If it is, we're going to call her Jani – as in Jan One, yeah?' She altered position on the sofa, reorganising the cushions. Her expression lost some of its animation. 'Judd still hasn't finished the nursery.'

'Ours were both boys.'

'Well, ours might be. I just call her "she" cos, I dunno, it feels like a she. Oh, *Jesus*.' Monica winced, easing herself onto the floor, kneeling, extending one leg behind her so that she resembled a sprinter in the starting blocks. Her words came out between sharp breaths. 'Cramp. Right... in... the... groin.'

The meal was ready, the Christmas message would begin in five minutes. Monica was still squatting, relieving her discomfort, in the middle of his living-room. From next door, there was the sound of something heavy being moved at speed across a floor, then a crack and the smashing of glass and a sentence comprised entirely of profanity.

'Coffee table,' Monica said. 'Or the telly.'

'You could watch the Queen here, with me, if you like.'

'D'you think you could help me up?'

Her hair was soft against his face and smelled faintly of

coconut. When he released his grip under her armpits, his palms were damp with the perspiration that had penetrated the fabric. She was crying again. They were only a short distance apart and Terence thought he should comfort her but, having just broken contact, he could not envisage the mechanics of it. He went out to the kitchen and turned the oven off. Outside, a red-and-white check teatowel hung on the line in the rain, saturated, almost translucent. He did not recall pegging it out.

'It's the hormones,' she said, when he returned to the room. She was standing by the wall dividing this house from hers. One hand was placed against it, just above the mantelpiece, as though she was testing for damp. 'Is this Violet?'

Terence saw the frame in her other hand. 'Yes.'

'I had a great aunt called Violet.' Monica continued to study the photograph then set it down again, out of position. 'Actually, no, it was Veronica.'

'We were married for forty-six years.'

'I can't imagine being together that long.'

'It doesn't seem long to me now,' Terence said. 'It seems like five minutes.'

She inclined her head to the wall, leaning closer, until her ear and both palms were pressed against it, but a silence had settled next door and after a moment she stepped back with a vague shake of the head. She crossed the room and retrieved the cigarette, rolling it between her thumb and middle finger, scrutinising it intently, as if the solution to a troublesome question was contained in the pattern of its motion.

'I should be getting back.'

'As I say, you'd be more than welcome—'

'All it is, right, is the reindeer stopped. They're supposed to move across the window.' She made an arc in the air with her hand. 'But they just stopped. One minute they're working, the next they're not. The lights are still on and everything. You know, the letters.' She placed the unlit cigarette between her lips and it twitched as she spoke. 'I said to him: *Judd, just leave it. It's fine. Just leave it.* But... nah.'

Terence didn't say anything.

'Everything has to be just right, with him.' Monica pinched the tip of her nose and he thought she was about to sneeze, then he saw that she was attempting to stop herself from crying again. 'He'll be in the fuse box now.'

'I expect so.'

She looked up. 'D'you have a light?'

'I don't smoke, I'm afraid.'

Monica nodded to herself. She remarked on the lack of a tree or decorations and Terence told her that they were bagged up in the loft and he hadn't bothered to bring them down this year. The cards on the mantelpiece were festive enough for him. He glanced at the clock, then at the television.

'I will stay and watch it with you,' she said. 'If that's okay.'

He smiled and switched the set on.

Good, she hadn't started yet. A continuity announcer was detailing some of the programmes scheduled for later in the day. The food would keep, Terence decided. It would be impolite to eat in front of his guest.

'Sit yourself down, then.'

There was a yelp from next door, a whoop, accompanied by a reiterative thumping on the wall – a clenched fist rather than a mallet, by the sound of it – and a distinct shout of: *Yes, yes, yes!*

Terence looked at Monica. She'd been on the point of lowering herself on to the sofa but rose again, hesitant and distracted.

'Mon!'

This, from the street. She went to the window and Terence saw her wave, then knock on the glass and wave again, grinning, mouthing silently.

'He wants me to go out and have a look.' Her uncertainty visibly returned now that she was facing into the room again.

She adjusted one of the clips in her hair. 'I think... I think I should probably go, actually. See to the turkey and that.'

Terence watched the Queen alone, eating his meal. He pulled the cracker and put the paper hat on his head. When it was all finished, he took the tray out to the kitchen along with the two sherry glasses and washed up.

He was stacking the second of the glasses in the draining rack when the letter flap opened and snapped shut. He shook the excess water from his hands and went along the hall. There was an envelope on the mat, with his name misspelled on the front. He opened it: a card, with an illustration of a robin perched on a snowman's carrot nose, signed *Monica and Judd (plus Jani!!!) XXX.* Judd was written in the same feminine hand as Monica. *P.S. Thanks a lot for the sherry!* Terence smiled. He read the inscription again and took the card through to the living-room and made space for it on the mantelpiece.

A Missing Person's Inquiry

OPENING THE INVESTIGATOR'S NOTEBOOK, and using the stubby pencil that came with it, Christie wrote down the things he remembered from the day his mother didn't come home. He listed them, as instructed, under three headings: 'Suspicous'; 'Unusual'; 'Ordinery'. But he wasn't sure of the difference between unusual and suspicious, so he tore out the page and started again. This time, just one list. With the strangest things at the top because they were the ones the police would be most interested in, probably.

1. Daddy told a big lie about mummy.
2. Daddy cryed.
3. I was taken out of numrasy to see Misses Dunken in her offis.
4. gran feched me from School before School was finish.
5. Daddy let me sleep with him.
6. I wet the bed.
7. mummy left in a Tacksy.
8. Nathans Mummy took me to school.

He was up to #19 (the clip on my lunch box brok) when there was a knock on the door and Grampa came in to say tea was ready. Grampa must've scratched his bald head again and made one of the scabs bleed. Christie closed the notebook and slotted the pencil in its spine and fitted them in their right places in the box.

'That any good?' Grampa said. His chin was sugary from not shaving.

Christie shrugged. 'Yeah.'

'I had something similar when I was a lad. Terry the Tec.'

He'd already told Christie this in Woolworths. Twenty pounds, they'd given him, Gran and Grampa. SuperSleuth cost £17.99 and he spent the rest on pick 'n' mix. Christie had to read some bits of the Detection Manual two or three times and still didn't know what all the words meant – but, then, he wasn't eight for another three months and the set was for boys of eleven or twelve, if the picture on the front was anything to go by. There was a Pressure Pad you slid under the carpet by the door so an alarm beeped if an intruder came into your room. But batteries weren't included, and Gran and Grampa didn't have any the right size.

'I've got a tummy ache,' Christie said.

'Well come down and see how much you can manage, eh?'

Staying at Gran and Grampa's by himself was unusual, but that happened the day after she went. Christie didn't put it on the list. He was in the room which used to be Mummy's. Her old books were there and her teddy, who was called Mr Cute, but it was like a grown-up's bedroom apart from that. It was just for a few days, to give Daddy a bit of space. Daddy phoned him the first evening, to say night-night, and the next morning; he promised to call every day and said that, before he knew it, Christie would be back home again.

'And Mummy?' he'd asked. But Daddy didn't want to talk about Mummy.

Why did he have to be sent away? There was loads of space for Daddy, even with him there. But Gran said there was so much to do 'at a time like this' and Daddy couldn't be expected to cope with him on top of everything else.

'I can dress myself,' Christie told her. 'And tie my laces.'

'I know you can, love.'

'I can make toast, now.'

★

'Do I have to go to school in the morning?' he asked at the tea table. Gran had given him chips, even though he'd told her he liked Smiley Faces better. Four fish fingers, though, instead of three, and she'd remembered about beans not peas.

'No,' Gran said. 'I've had a word with Mrs Duncan and she says you don't have to go back just yet.'

He thought of Daddy, in the house by himself. Probably he wouldn't go out at all but just wait inside. In case Mummy came back, or tried to phone. Or if the man who took her called to ask for money. Or so the detectives would know where Daddy was if they needed to talk to him.

'Are they looking for him?'

Gran frowned. Her and Grampa were eating fish pie, not fingers. Mum's Fish Pie, Mummy called it. The steam misted up Gran's glasses each time she bent over the plate to eat. 'Looking for who?' she said.

'The taxi driver.'

Gran looked at Grampa. Christie thought one of them would say something, but they didn't. They just went on eating. He pushed his plate away. Said he'd had enough, although he'd only eaten half a fish finger, a few beans and none of the chips.

Later, on his way to the toilet, Christie thought he heard a puppy in the big bedroom, whimpering to be let out. But Gran and Grampa didn't have a puppy. He listened a bit longer and realised it was Gran making the noise. Grampa was in there, too, mumbling to her. Christie couldn't make out any of the words.

He opened up SuperSleuth and took out the Photo-Fit Cards. They had an oval for the face and there were sticker sheets of hair, eyes, eyebrows, mouths, noses, chins, ears, beards, moustaches and glasses that stuck on and peeled off. Drawn ones, not photos.

Christie tried to remember the taxi driver's face.

Nathan and his mummy had been on their doorstep. Mummy hurried Christie over, checked that he had his lunch-box and book-bag, kissed him bye-bye and went back to the taxi. Nathan's Mummy shouted 'Good luck!' Mummy was in her smart clothes and had a black briefcase instead of her shoulder bag. He should tell the police about that; it might be significantly ordinary or even unusual. The driver's face was turned their way, watching Mummy as she crossed the road and got in the back. Then he faced the front and drove off. Mummy waved. Christie didn't want to wave back in front of Nathan. He wished he had, now. Wished she'd hugged him bye-bye, not just kissed his cheek.

'I bet she brings you back something nice,' Nathan's Mummy had said.

But Christie just gave a shrug. He hadn't been to London and was still cross with Mummy for not taking him with her.

He chose a brown oval. It wasn't quite the right brown but the other brown one was even darker, more like black people's brown than Indian people's. After trying out different features, he finally had a face that was almost how he remembered the taxi driver's. The detectives would put it in the newspapers and on the telly. If he'd had SuperSleuth that morning, he could've made a note of the number plate. Except he probably wouldn't have thought to because the taxi driver wasn't suspicious, then, and Mummy wasn't gone. The taxi was white, with a green diagonal stripe on the driver's door. He wrote that down in his Investigator's Notebook.

They would need a photograph of Mummy, too. For the news. So that if anyone spotted her with the taxi driver they'd know it was her and dial 999. Probably, Daddy had already given them one. In case he'd forgotten, Christie decided to get one of the pictures of her from the sideboard, where Gran and

Grampa kept family photos in silvery frames, as well as the painting Christie did of a triceratops. Dad called it a biceratops, because it only had two horns.

'Gran, can I have a picture of Mummy please? To take upstairs.'

He'd found her in the kitchen, just standing there, staring out the window at the back garden. It was raining. She half-turned towards him. 'A picture?'

'A photograph,' Christie said. 'From the sideboard.'

She was staring at him now, but not the way she'd been staring at the garden. She made her face soft and put her arms round him, gently, as though she was afraid of hurting him. Her cardigan was scratchy against his cheek. 'Christie love, of course you can have a picture of Mummy. Let's go and choose one, shall we?'

It had to be a recent one, he told her.

The second day, at Gran and Grampa's, Christie dusted for fingerprints. They'd stayed here at Christmas, which wasn't that long ago, and he reckoned Mummy's fingerprints would still be on things. In the bedroom where she and Daddy slept, he dusted the door handle, the knob on the wardrobe door, the picture of him as a baby which he remembered her picking up from the window ledge to show him. Other places, too. He found lots of fingerprints. Trouble was, he couldn't tell which were Mummy's and which were Daddy's. Maybe Gran and Grampa came in here as well sometimes, or Uncle John and Auntie Kath might have stayed in this room since Christmas. Some of the prints were bigger than others. Christie decided they must be men's. Or thumbs.

He went downstairs. Grampa was in the lounge, watching the news. He switched it off as soon as Christie entered the room. Usually, Christie was allowed to watch TV when they stayed here but this time he wasn't. Only DVDs.

'Grampa,' he said, 'can I take your fingerprints, please?'

Grampa looked at the Ink Pad and Fingerprint Cards in Christie's hands. For a moment, Christie though he'd ask why, or just say no, but after a bit Grampa smiled and got out of his chair and cleared some space on the coffee table.

'I'll put a magazine under, eh Sherlock?, so we don't get into trouble.'

Christie held Grampa's hands the way it said to and pressed the tip of each finger and thumb on the pad then rolled them in the squares on one of the cards. He did Gran's, too. She was knocking up some sandwiches for their lunch (she said he could have jam, which he wasn't allowed at home) and he had to wait for her to finish before taking her prints. Christie wanted to go straight back upstairs to compare Gran and Grampa's prints against the ones he'd dusted for. But he had to sit and eat first.

In the middle of lunch the phone rang. Grampa answered. He told the caller to hold on a sec then took the phone out into the hall and closed the door behind him.

'Look at that,' Gran said. She pointed at the half-eaten sandwich on Grampa's plate, which had a grey oval smudge on the bread where he hadn't washed his hands.

Upstairs, after lunch, Christie pressed a strip of sticky tape over a print he was pretty sure belonged to his mother and transferred it carefully on to one of the special plasticky blue Fingerprint Sheets you could hold up to the light.

He studied the swirly pattern. It looked as though it ought to glow in the dark.

Christie wasn't sure how it would help the police. Perhaps if they found the taxi, they'd have to dust for prints, or the place where he was keeping her, and they'd need to know what her prints looked like. No two people had the same fingerprints, the Detection Manual said. It was odd to think of Mummy, being missing somewhere, when her fingerprints were still here, in Gran and Grampa's house.

'Would you like to come down and have a game of something?' Gran said, one afternoon. It was the third or fourth day.

'No thank you.'

'How about if I put on one of your videos?'

'They're DVDs.'

'A DVD, then.'

'No thank you. I'm all right up here.'

The day before, she'd come in and sat beside him on the bed and held his hand and talked to him about what happened to Mummy. It was the same lie Daddy told. This time she didn't come in. She just gave him an odd sort of smile then left, shutting the door quietly, like Mummy did when she thought he was asleep.

He hadn't wet the bed, here.

He was too old to wet the bed. The other night, when he wet the bed at home, he took his pyjamas off and put them in the laundry basket in the bathroom and dried himself with a towel. He took the wet sheet off the bed. The duvet cover was damp, too, so he pulled that off. But he didn't know where the clean sheets and things were kept. Also, the mattress had a big wet patch. Daddy must've heard him moving around by then and came into the bedroom.

'You had an accident?' he said.

'Yeah.'

They stared at the mattress together. Daddy looked like he was asleep standing up. He said: 'D'you want to come in with me, in the big bed?'

'Can I?' Christie tried to remember the last time he'd been allowed to do that. He would've been five or six, probably.

'Come on, Chris. I'll sort you out some fresh pyjamas.'

He hardly ever called him Chris. He called him Monkey, or Chimp. That was something else unusual, now he thought about it. Christie slept on Mummy's side. A book was on the bedside table with a tassly bookmark poking out, and one of the stick things she cleaned her ears with, and a nearly empty glass of water. Her fluffy dressing gown was hanging on a hook on the back of the door. Daddy turned off the light. Mummy's side of the bed was cold. Christie moved his arms and legs about to warm it up. He thought Daddy was already asleep, but when he snuggled up to him Daddy rolled over and cuddled him back. He smelled of sweat and breath and old pyjamas.

'Are we still moving to London?' Christie said.

Right after that, Daddy started shaking. It was the same as when he laughed, but it wasn't laughing it was crying. One of the tears plopped on to Christie's face. It tasted of salt. He hadn't seen Daddy cry before.

Grampa took him to the park, the day it stopped raining. The detectives still hadn't come to question Christie and he was worried they might call while he was out. But Grampa said it would do him good to get some fresh air and a bit of exercise. Christie went on the swings and climbed the rope pyramid and used the digger thing, but it was a school day and the only other children there were toddlers or babies and he felt silly.

Afterwards, Christie had a cone from the kiosk next to the café and Grampa had a coffee and they sat on a picnic bench outside, even though it was cold. He liked this park. There was a river, with ducks. In summer there was a bouncy castle.

'Did you bring Mummy here when she was a girl?'

Grampa took a sip of his drink; his breath, when he spoke, came out white like cigarette smoke. 'Aye, she loved this place.'

Neither of them said anything for a while. Christie sucked the ice-cream into a tall, pointy shape like a volcano and dipped the tip of his tongue in the top to make a crater. He wished he hadn't already licked off the raspberry sauce because that could have been the lava. He showed it to Grampa, who said it was very good.

Then Christie told him about the taxi driver, and how he was the last person to see Mummy and about how significant that was in a missing person's inquiry.

'Christie –' Grampa put his coffee down. Placed his hands either side of it, the backs of his leather gloves wrinkling like old brown skin.

'What?'

Grampa looked at him. Then he looked away, towards the river. His fleece hat was like blue hair and his eyelids were pink from the wind. 'Nothing,' he said, at last. 'Look, I don't know about you, but I'm frozen sitting here. Eh? Finish that off and we'll get home and in the warm.'

Back indoors, Christie went to hang up his coat while Grampa struggled on the doorstep with his laces. The peg was just too high and he pulled down a couple of other coats and a scarf trying to reach. He picked up the scarf. It was bright red and made of stuff that looked prickly but was actually really soft. It was Mummy's. At first, Christie couldn't work out how it came to be there and he thought she must've turned up while he and Grampa were at the park. Then he remembered her saying she'd lost her scarf and how Daddy would be upset because it was a birthday present and cost a lot of money. But she hadn't lost it. It was here all along, from when they'd stayed at Christmas, probably.

Christie pressed the scarf to his face. It smelled of Mummy's perfume.

If the police used sniffer dogs, the scarf would give them a scent to follow. Christie folded it flat in the bottom of the SuperSleuth box, beneath the plastic tray, along with the photo of Mummy from the sideboard. That was when he noticed something else, shiny in the light: a hair, stuck to the scarf. A long, gingery hair that curled in the middle. He used the Tweezers to remove it and laid it on a blank page from the notebook, careful not to breathe too hard in case it blew away.

Under the Magnifying Glass, the hair was lots of colours all at once; at one end, it split in two. When he was done with examining the hair, Christie taped it to a card and put it in an Evidence Bag.

mummies hare, he wrote on the label.

From this, they'd be able to determine her DNA. Christie didn't know what 'determine' meant, or exactly what DNA was – but he understood enough to realise it was significant. If the police found a hair the same as this on the taxi driver's clothes it would incriminate him. Christie put the Evidence Bag in the box.

One morning, Christie came downstairs to find Auntie Kath in the kitchen with Gran and a woman Gran said was Irene from next door. They were making sandwiches and putting them on plates on the dining table along with sausages on sticks and cheese and pineapple and mini-sausage rolls and a huge pork pie cut into slices and bowls of crisps and peanuts. Auntie Kath gave him a hug that lifted him off his feet.

'Are we having a party?' Christie said.

His aunt went on hugging him, rocking him. 'Oh, Christie, sweetheart.' She put him down. Held his face between her hands. 'How are you doing, young man?'

'Where are Ben and Amy?'

Ben and Amy were his big cousins. Ben was nearly grown up, but Amy was twelve and didn't mind playing with Christie.

'They'll be along later, pet.'

It was busy in the kitchen. He wanted to help put things on sticks, but Gran said: 'Why don't you go and say hello to your Uncle John, there's a good lad.'

Uncle John was in the lounge with Grampa. There were cans of beer in a stack on the floor by his chair, in cardboard trays wrapped in plastic. Both men were wearing suits. His uncle's face had been serious but when he saw Christie he put on a big grin.

'Now, then!' he said, pulling Christie onto his lap for some rough and tumble.

It was important to compile a timeline, to put all the events into their chronological sequence, as far as it could be reliably established. The investigation team could then assemble a storyboard of the who, what, where, when. Any inconsistencies in the witnesses' statements would become evident.

Christie wished he'd read this bit before making his list of unusual, suspicious and ordinary things. Now he'd have to write them all out again, in a different order. He worked on it in his room while the grown-ups got everything ready downstairs. The problem was he couldn't tell the time, unless it was exactly something o'clock. Also, there were two timelines: the one that happened, and the one Mummy told him would happen.

That morning, when she was getting him ready to go over to Nathan's, she talked him through the day so he could picture where she'd be while he was at school.

'When Miss Scowcroft takes the register, I'll just be getting on the train,' she said. Mummy was washing grapes for his lunch-box, talking over her shoulder as she stood at the sink. 'And by the time my train reaches London, you'll be at playtime.'

'What's after that?'

'You have numeracy before lunch on a Monday, don't you?'

'I think so.'

'Okay, while you're in numeracy, I'll be going into my interview.'

'Is that when they give you the job?'

Mummy laughed. 'Not right there and then, no.'

'Then will you come home?'

'Well, I have to do a presentation as well — a kind of talk — so it'll go on for a bit.' She held up a Time Out and a Twix.

Christie pointed at the Twix and she popped it in his lunch-box and clipped it shut, only the clip snapped off (Mummy said the S-word) and she had to use sticky tape to keep it closed. 'So,' she said, 'I won't be getting the train home until about half-past three, just as you're coming out of school.'

'And Nathan's Mummy is collecting me as well as taking me.'

'That's right. And after you and Nathan have had tea and a bit of a play, I'll be back.' Mummy was sorting through his book-bag. They hadn't practised his spellings, she said, but it didn't matter because the test wasn't till Wednesday. 'You going to be okay?' she said, stroking his hair.

'Does Nathan's Mummy know I don't like peas any more?'

Christie was in his room, putting on the clothes Gran had given him: his dark grey school trousers and white shirt, and a black blazer he hadn't seen before and which looked new and had a shiny lining that was cold to the touch. The tie was Grampa's; navy-blue with black diamonds. As he had another go at tying it, there were footsteps on the landing then a double-knock. He thought it might be the police.

'Chimp, you in there?'

'Daddy!'

The door opened and there was Daddy, all smart like he was going to work, but he didn't mind when Christie jumped up and hung from his neck. His face smelled of the lemony shaving foam he used and which made Christie think of meringue.

'You're making a right pig's ear of this,' Daddy said, loosening Christie's tie and doing it up properly. He asked Christie how he was and Christie said fine and they hugged again and Daddy said he'd missed him and it was good to see him and Christie said he'd missed Daddy too.

'Are we going home now?'

'Not right this minute,' Daddy said. 'But later. This evening.'

Daddy's face was tired. Like it was that time he'd drunk too much wine and was being sick in the bathroom the next morning when Christie went in for a wee.

'Can I show you SuperSleuth?' Christie said. Daddy looked confused. He led him over to the bed, where the box was, and took out the pieces to show him: the Investigator's Notebook, the Magnifying Glass, the Fingerprint Cards. 'This is one of Mummy's hairs.' He held the Evidence Bag for Daddy to see. He was about to explain about the scarf, but Daddy interrupted.

'Chimp, please. Don't.'

'Here's a photograph of Mummy,' Christie said. 'And this is him.'

Daddy looked at the Photo-Fit Card. 'Who?'

'The *taxi driver.*' He'd told Daddy about him on the phone at least twice and Daddy had forgotten already. 'We have to give this to the police so they can–'

'Okay, Chris, enough. That's *enough.*'

Gran was in the doorway. Christie didn't know she was there until she spoke. Her voice sounded like a whisper after theirs. 'Michael, the cars will be here soon.'

Daddy didn't answer. He just stood there, his head tipped down like it was too heavy for his neck. After a moment, he pulled Christie into another hug.

Gran had a little job for Christie. The dressing-table stool in Gran and Grampa's room needed taking down to the dining room. And mind not to chip the wall on the stairs.

She stayed in his bedroom with Daddy. He heard their voices behind the shut door as he carried the stool across the landing.

The other grown-ups were in the lounge, by the sound of it. Apart from Uncle John, who was out on the front step, smoking. In the dining room, the table with all the food was against the far wall and the chairs had been set out in a big circle, along with the two armchairs from the lounge and an old yellowy-brown chair he recognised from the second bedroom. There was no space for his stool. Christie put it down. He jiggled a couple of the other chairs along a bit to make a gap. One of the armchairs got stuck – Grampa's, with the holey arm-rests – and he lifted it up to find that a caster was jammed. He popped it back under its wheel.

Now, the seat-cushion had fallen off.

Which was when Christie saw the newspaper that had been stashed underneath. It had Mummy's picture on the front, and another one of a car.

The car was upside down with firemen all around it. It was squashed against a lorry and one of the wheels was sticking out. If it wasn't for the diagonal green stripe Christie wouldn't have known it was a taxi. Lower down the page were two smaller pictures: Mummy's face, when her hair was shorter; and the taxi driver.

Christie read the words, the big ones along the top. Daddy's lie, again.

He put the cushion back, on top of the newspaper so he couldn't see it any more. But the pictures were still in his head. The upside-down taxi. Mummy, smiling so her teeth showed. Her slice-of-melon smile, Daddy called it. The taxi driver wasn't smiling. His lips were a thin line beneath his moustache. He didn't look like Christie remembered. The eyes were the wrong shape. The eyebrows. And the hair wasn't as big. Later, before Daddy took him home, Christie would have to go back upstairs and do the Photo-Fit again or the detectives would never catch him.

Unsaid

FEBRUARY 17th

04.38

    ...
    ...
    'Oh, Dad, you poor bugger.'
    ...
    ...
    ...
    ...

04.30

'Mrs Read?'
    'Yes, he just... I think he's... I don't think he's...'
    'Let me take a look.'

February 16th

23.51

'You're still here.'
    'It's okay, I'm just going to sit with you for a bit.'
    'Please don't, love.'
    'Shh, shh, it's okay. Don't upset yourself.'
    ...

'What time is it?'
'I don't know. Late.'
'I'm so fucking tired.'
'Sleep, then. I'll sit here while you sleep.'
...
...
'Go home, Est.'
'I'm not going anywhere.'
'I don't fucking want you here.'

21.47

'You shouldn't have to do this.'
   'Keep still or it'll go everywhere.'
   'Where's the nurse? This should be her –'
   'Dad, keep *still.*'

19.19

'They've let a gipsy family in.'
   'What?'
   'They let them camp in the fucking ward, if you can believe it.'
   'Don't pull that off.'
   'I can't talk with –'
   'Here, let me –'
   'Fucking thing.'
   'There.'
   ...
   ...
   'Can you speak to someone?'
   'You have to keep the mask on.'
   'About the gipsies. They won't listen to me.'
   ...
   'They've no right to be on the ward.'
   'No.'

...

...

'Have you got the biscuits?'
'Yes, I've got them.'
'They were just here. Where −'
'I've got them. Don't worry about the biscuits.'

18.06

'If there are any friends or family who want to see him, they should come in this evening.'

...

'I'm very sorry.'

...

...

'But... he was up and about just a couple of days ago.'
'I know, I know.'
'Up and down the corridor.'

...

'Flirting with the nurses.'
'That's how it is, sometimes, Mrs Read, I'm sorry to say.'

...

...

'He was going into Beckside.'
'Was he?'
'You know, the one on Crossmoor Road. Just till the extension was ready.'

...

'He used to be a blood donor. Fifty-five donations.'
'Did he? Fifty-five. Well, that's remarkable, it really is.'

18.02

'Excuse me, Mr Pacey. Mrs Read, do you have a moment?'
'Yes. Yes, of course.'
'You off, Est?'

'I'm just going to have a word with the doctor. Okay? I'll be back in a sec.'

'Did you remember the biscuits?'

'I'm not going yet. I'll just talk to Dr Vora and come right back.'

'They were here somewhere.'

'You already gave them to me. Look.'

'I told that fucking woman I can't swallow anything solid.'

'I won't be long, Dad.'

'They'll only get thrown.'

…

'Let's find somewhere we can sit down and talk, shall we?'

'Yes. Thank you, doctor.'

17.59

'This is all a bit rubbish, isn't it?'

'Eh?'

'This. You.'

…

'The nurse said you had a bad night.'

'Which nurse?'

'The pretty one.'

'She's from Srinagar.'

'Sri Lanka, not Srinagar.'

'Srinagar. That's right. *Ceylon*, in my day.'

…

…

'Your hair needs cutting.'

'They don't bother with that. Hair, toenails. D'you want these? I told the tea lady I didn't want them but I might as well talk to my fucking self.'

'Mind your IV.'

'What?'

'Your drip. You'll pull it out.'

'Here. Custard Creams.'

'I don't want them.'

'Go on. They'll only get thrown.'

17.54

'Have you seen him yet?'

'No, I've just this minute come in.'

'Only, we've been trying to call you.'

'Call me?'

'Dr Vora wants to speak to you.'

'Why, what's happened?'

'You pop down to see your dad and I'll let Dr Vora know you're here.'

February 14th

13.20

'Beckside rang this morning. They wondered if I could get hold of a list of Dad's medication before he's discharged.'

'We can get that for you, Mrs Read. I'll have a word with one of the doctors.'

February 12th

16.45

'What's this?'

'It's the house.'

'Whose house?'

'Ours, you numpty. Mine and Charles's. Look, here's where you'll be.'

'The garage?'

'No, *that's* the garage. This bit here. The extension.'

'I didn't know you'd built an extension.'

'We haven't, yet. Blimey, keep up, eh?'

…

...
'You draw these, did you?'
'Yeah.'
'Couldn't find a ruler, then?'
'Ha-di-ha.'
...
...
'You'll lose a lot of garden.'

February 10th

13.25

'You can give it more welly than that, Est.'
'I don't want to nick you.'
'It's not an armpit.'
'It'd be a lot easier if you didn't keep talking.'
...
...
'You're just scraping the foam off.'
'*Dad.*'
...
...
...
'Makes a lovely sound, doesn't it? Like Velcro.'
...
'Doing anything nice at the weekend, sir?'
'Heh.'

February 6th

14.57

'How you doing today?'
'No, not good. Not really.'
...

...

'I hear you had a bit of a to-do in the night.'

'A to-do was it?'

'What happened, then?'

'I needed the toilet.'

'Uh-huh.'

'No-one comes. You press the buzzer, but it might as well not be wired up for all the notice anyone takes. I'm sitting here like a prize fucking lemon.'

'Why didn't you just go across the way, Dad?'

'It's these legs.'

'So, what hap –'

'No bedpan, of course. They take one away and you'll get another in a day or two, if they can be bothered.'

'The ward sister said you did it on a newspaper.'

'I buzz and buzz and no bastard comes – am I meant to just shit in the bed?'

...

...

'Okay, Dad. It's okay.'

'Fuckers. Bloody fuckers.'

14.54

'When the nurse went in there to clean him up, I'm afraid your father became quite abusive.'

'Did he?'

'I won't have my staff being spoken to like that.'

'No. Of course not.'

February 5th

16.00

'What happened to that old boy in the bed opposite?'

'What d'you think happened to him?'

...
...
...
'It's lovely out there today.'
...
'Charles sends his love. And the girls.'
...
...
'His daughter was in earlier. Emptying out his cabinet.'
...
...
'I'll top up your water, will I?'

January 31st

11.24

'She seemed nice.'
  'Who?'
  'Dr Bhandiwal.'
  'Never seen her before. You get a different one every time.'
...
...
'Why didn't you tell me before?'
'Before what?'
'Before now.'
...
...
'If Mrs Court downstairs hadn't–'
'You've got your own life. The house. Charles. The girls.
Your job.'
  'You're part of my life, too, Dad. In case you'd forgotten.'
...
'I just wish you'd said something sooner.'
'Yeah, well. You're here now.'

'I could've been here sooner. You might not have got into this state.'

'Could've, might've. Esther, love, I haven't learned much in eighty years but I know you can't pay any visits to yesterday.'

'Wish I had a quid for every time you've told me that.'

'Doesn't make it any less true.'

11.18

'Frankly, what I'm going to say is that we need to admit you, Mr Pacey. Let them take a good look at you over at St Dunstan's.'

'Admit him?'

'Yes, Mrs Read, I think so. I think we need to do that.'

'What, today?'

'Yes. I'll call them now.'

…

…

'How d'you feel about that, Dad?'

'About what?'

'Going into hospital.'

08.42

'Who was that?'

'The doctor's. I've got you an appointment – 11 o'clock.'

'What d'you want to go and do that for?'

January 30th

21.52

'I do wish you hadn't come, Est.'

'Thank you. Don't mention it.'

'You should be with the girls.'

'Yeah, right. We mostly communicate by text anyway these days, even when we're all in the same building.'

...

...

'You look like you could do with an early night yourself.'

'That line might work on some women, Dad.'

...

'Woah, steady there. You okay?'

'It's just when I bend over. Or stand up suddenly.'

'You're all shaky.'

'It'll be the shaking that causes that.'

...

...

'Here, let me... there we go.'

'You're very good, you know.'

'I'm sure you tucked me in a few times.'

'Not me. Your mother did all that. Bath-time, bedtime. Meals. Nappies. I was just there for the tickle-fights and the dad-jokes.'

'They were *jokes*?'

19.34

'I am capable of washing up, you know.'

'I'm sure you are. But I'm not seeing a lot of evidence of it, to be honest.'

'Why don't you hoover while you're here?'

'Do you even own a hoover?'

'And I expect the bath could do with a good scrub.'

'Rubber gloves? Flash? J-cloths?'

'Don't know how I've managed on my own all this time.'

'Dad, this place is like a biology experiment.'

'There's a B&B down the road if it's not to your liking.'

...

...

'Sorry. I didn't come here to squabble.'

'Where d'you normally go to do that, then?'

19.06

'So, what're the other people here like?'

'Don't have much to do with them, if I can help it. Apart from your woman downstairs. No avoiding her. Mrs N. Bloody-Parker.'

'She's only looking out for you.'

'Is that what you call it?'

…

'What about work, love?'

'I had a few days holiday owing.'

'A few days?'

'Fraid so.'

…

…

'You can't go traipsing up and down the country every time I bloody sneeze.'

…

…

'You not hungry?'

'Not really.'

…

…

'You look like you've lost a lot of weight, Dad.'

15.47

'I'll put the kettle on, will I?'

'Check the milk first.'

…

…

'Technically, that's cottage cheese.'

'I don't mind it black. Nice and strong. Just leave the bag in.'

'Strong enough to stand your spoon up?'

'Something like that, yeah.'

…

...
...

'I don't like the sound of that cough.'

'So don't listen to it.'

15.42

'You've got a nice bit of garden, Dad.'

'I've not been down yet.'

'But, to look at. And in the spring – it'll be lovely out there, then.'

...

'D'you remember the sunflowers we grew? You and me.'

'Eh?'

'The sunflowers. At Leigham Road.'

'I remember you getting all upset when they died off.'

'I'd have been, what – seven, eight?'

'Something like that.'

'You loved that garden, you and Mum.'

'We did.'

'Your *patch*.'

'I do remember that summer we had courgettes with every meal for a month, just to use them up.'

'Oh, yeah. God, we did. Or was it marrow?'

'I thought it was courgettes.'

'Maybe it was. It's a long–'

'No, you're right, love. It was marrow.'

...
...
...

'Didn't you win a prize one year for biggest marrow?'

'Heh. Where's Frankie Howerd when you need him?'

15.31

'What the bloody hell are you doing here?'

'Hello, Dad – nice to see you, too.'

'You drove all this way?'

'Looks like it.'

...

...

'She rang you, didn't she? Bloody warden.'

'You can take the chain off, if you like. I might struggle to come in otherwise.'

'I've got no food in.'

'Just as well I swung by Tesco on the way, then, isn't it?'

'You could've phoned.'

'You could try checking your voicemail.'

...

...

'You've done your hair different.'

'Blimey, well done, Dad – Charles hasn't even noticed and it's been three days.'

...

...

'What did she say about me?'

'Never mind who said what. I'm here, that's all.'

'An invasion of privacy is what it is.'

'Oh give over, Dad.'

...

...

'I suppose you'd better come in.'

January 29th

20.14

'It's for you, E.'

    'Who is it?'

    'Mrs Cork?'

    'Cork?'

    'That's what it sounded like. Litchbury number.'

'Oh. Okay.'

…

…

…

'Hello, Esther Read speaking.'

A Representative in Automotive Components

1. My Cousin is Kissing

ON THE APPROACH TO Jodhpur, Nathan bolted himself in the WC. He assumed the roll and pitch of the train, shifting weight from one foot to the other; sipping shallow breaths of stench. Through the vent in the floor, the track spooled beneath him, the wheels filling his head with their clatter. It was hot in the cubicle; not sauna-hot but dry like an oven. He swallowed. The illness wasn't fully upon him, but there was a headache, queasiness, a sense of his body recoiling from itself.

He took off his baggy cheesecloth shirt, raised the T-shirt he wore underneath, and checked the integrity of each of the parcels strapped to his torso. The tape had come unstuck in places but the polythene wrappings appeared to be intact. There was no mirror to examine the ones on his back and he didn't dare unpeel everything in there to take a proper look. He made do with repairing the tape as best he could, then lowered his T-shirt again and pulled the other shirt back on. Done. He tidied his clothes. Composed himself. This was okay, he could handle this.

Back in his seat, Nathan evaded a smile of incipient conversation from the passenger sitting opposite. Outside, dirt tracks gave way to streets, shanties to squat cubes of white, the buildings amplifying the day's brilliance. Jodhpur materialised like a city sculpted from salt.

He took an auto-rickshaw, naming the hotel for the driver; he knew it wasn't far but he was too tired to walk, too jaded to wade through the touts picketing the station concourse. Unwashed, unshaven, unslept; stiff from sitting for so long on a bare wooden seat. His skeleton had absorbed every vibration of the ten-hour journey, transmuting general discomfort into a dull pulse of pain at the base of his spine. The arrival was familiar: odours of sewage and burnt ghee; cars, cycles, mopeds, buses, trucks and auto-rickshaws reeling by on fast-forward, patterning the air with beige dust, din and petrol fumes. On seething pavements, all the men wore white and the women were swathed in psychedelic orange, yellow, cerise – the colours of the spices heaped on street-side stalls. The tape tugged at his skin with each jolt of the vehicle. Nathan closed his eyes, opened them again, focusing on the vest – translucent with sweat – stretched taut across the driver's back. At the hotel, the man hauled the pack inside before Nathan could stop him. He spoke Hindi to the desk clerk.

'Driver says he tells you 'bout my hotel.'

Nathan made the cash sign with his fingers. 'He's trying it on.'

The clerk and the driver quarrelled, their voices pressing like thumbs into Nathan's eye sockets. He craved sleep and warmth and wellness. Two nights, there. Whatever he was coming down with, he would have to take with him, to Delhi, for the meeting with the German. She was the one who had told him about this hotel. *Indians, mostly. You stay where Westerners stay, it is a risk.* A four-storey colonial building fronting onto a plaza kaleidoscopic with traffic. Grime mottled the stone fascia and, over the entrance, the hotel name had weathered from red to pale pink. The lobby smelled of turmeric and something sweetly indecipherable. Nathan looked around for a chair. There wasn't one. As he filled in the register, sweat leaked from his forehead, smudging the ink. The clerk transcribed passport details into a ledger, and there were the usual forms to complete. In his head, Nathan counted to ten and back down again.

'Rooms are thirty rupees and forty rupees. In forty-rupee room you have personal WC, shower.'

'I'll take a forty-rupee room.'

The clerk inspected the ledger, shaking his head. 'Sorry, no awailability.' He returned the passport and shouted. A boy appeared: skinny, ten or twelve years old, wearing a white vest and dhoti and blue plastic flip-flops. More Hindi. The boy detached a key from a panel of hooks on the wall behind the counter and signalled Nathan to give him his pack. It was almost as big as the boy, chafing his calves as he heaved it up one flight of stairs after another. He said his name was Anil.

Nathan spoke through dredged breath. 'No lift?'

'Lift broken.'

The room was on the top floor, at the end of a long balcony. Engine noise, klaxons and a tannoy-blare of music levitated from below like audible heat-haze. There was a time when he'd have paused for a photo, or just to gaze out across the rooftops.

'American?' the boy asked.

'English.'

'Where are you coming from?'

'Today? Jaisalmer.'

'You are having camel ride?'

Nathan removed a trainer and shook it to release a dusting of sand. Anil liked that. He had shouldered the pack against the wall beside a brown door and was jiggling the key into the lock. Nathan asked about the toilets and showers. *Number three level*. The bed was unmade, there was a lightbulb set into one wall, a bedside table, a wash-basin crazed with cracks, a wooden chair and curtains that were drawn closed, dousing the room in an anaemic green glow. The floor was bare concrete.

Nathan pointed to the bed. 'No mosquito net?'

A grin, a wag of the head. Nathan made a whining noise and jerked his fingers. *Acha!* The boy separated the curtains to disclose a mesh screen mended with strips of sticking plaster. He searched Nathan's face for approval. Then he switched on the ceiling fan, distributing shadows about the walls. The blades ticked loudly and gave off a smell of scorched metal, the erratic downdraught making the curtains dance. Nathan pressed a note into the boy's hand and asked him to fetch tea and bottled water.

'My cousin is kissing.'

'No girls.'

'You like boy?'

'No boys.'

As soon as Anil had gone, Nathan stripped off all the packages and stowed them under the bed, taping them to the underside of the wire webbing that supported the mattress. Not ideal, but it would have to do. It was a relief not to be wearing them anymore. His skin was covered with rectangular pink blotches and flecks of tape-gum.

He was unpacking the rest of his things when the boy returned. The tea tasted excessively sweet, as it always did in India. There were biscuits in his pack, but he couldn't face them. When had he last eaten? Jaisalmer. A carton of glutinous dhal and rice from a vendor. Soon he would be eating Western food again. Home in a clean, crisp land where his senses no longer flinched from constant intrusion. He imagined himself at Indira Gandhi, in a few days, money-belt so taut with dollar bills it would nip the flesh as he lowered himself into his seat on the plane. Patience, composure, focus – that way, the days divided into hours and minutes until you could almost feel their passing. He spoke aloud to the empty room: *Do not blow this.*

Within minutes of finishing his drink, Nathan puked into the basin – no vomit, just a warm splash of tea. He sat on the bed for a long time, shivering, dampening the sheet with his sweat.

2. The Bucket

He was trapped underwater, a rescue party at the surface playing searchlight beams across the seabed. His eyes bulged. His chest, his head, pounded with the pressure; limbs so laden with waterlogged clothing he couldn't... a persistent knocking, a voice. *Hello, English!* Morning spilled into his room through rents in the curtains. The voice, again. Anil. Nathan swung his legs out of bed and, sitting up too abruptly, had to suppress a surge of nausea. The T-shirt and shorts clung to him as though he'd been shrink-wrapped. He hung his head between his knees, then raised it, shoving damp hair back from his forehead. Still, the knocking.

'English? Please, open.'

'I don't want any breakfast.'

Anil gave three sharp raps. 'You cup, please.'

Nathan swore. He carried the tea cup from the previous afternoon across the room and yanked the door open. Daylight shrouded the boy in a fluorescent corona that rendered his teeth and clothes supernaturally white.

'Problem?'

'No problem.' Nathan blocked the doorway. 'I was sleeping.'

'Breakfast? Paratha, jam, tea, boil egg, shamble egg, dhal, banana. You what?'

'Nothing. No, okay, bananas.' He held up two fingers.

The stool was the loosest so far, like melted chocolate. It took several minutes to accumulate in the depression between the foot-rests. He used the scoop to flush, then on himself, the cold douche hurting like a bruise. Raising himself from squat position, his knees gave and he had to brace himself against the wall. When Nathan returned from the toilets, he found the brown door to his room ajar even though he had locked it. An old woman was sweeping the floor, stooping to reach under the bed with long scything motions. She became flustered at his appearance, drawing the headscarf of her sari across her mouth.

'No cleaning now.' He gestured towards the door. 'Go away.'

She pressed her palms together as she hurried out. 'Namaste.'

Nathan checked the parcels. All still in place. On the floor under the bed was a matchstick, the tinfoil plinth and fragmented ash of a spent mosquito-coil, and a dead cockroach big as a thumb, all gathered in a mound of dust. He surprised himself with his revulsion. Weeks back, in a dorm in Varanasi, he'd passed an hour with two Kiwis watching ants dismantle a roach corpse, segment by segment, and carry it away.

Nathan sipped from the bottle. The bananas, he left uneaten on the table. He tried to shave, but there was no hot water and even the lowering of his face over the basin made his head ache so much he had to sit down until the pain abated. It made him fearful, what was happening to his body – afraid of the illness, but also of the consequences of failing to deliver. When she'd declared his fee, the German had smiled, then ceased smiling. *Don't do this only for reward, Nathan. We prefer you to think also of the – penalty? – yes, the penalty of neglecting your obligation.*

A day, another night, another morning; then, taxi-train-taxi-hotel. Delhi. Job done. Once the delivery was made he could be as sick as he liked.

He needed the toilet again. One of the Kiwis reckoned you could time the intervals between shits, as a woman marks contractions during labour; Nathan forgot the calculation, but it was supposed to help diagnose proximity to death.

He occupied his bed, perspiring, sleeping or not sleeping, coughing, observing the rotations of the ceiling fan, waiting for Anil. Regularly, urgently, he took himself to the third floor. Hours were no longer calibrated by minutes but by these shuffling excursions to the toilets. The bananas turned brown then black on his bedside table; a plain biscuit was expelled, soon after its consumption, in undigested chunks. If he drank anything more than a sip of water he retched it back up with such vehemence that he couldn't breathe until the spasm ceased. In the evening, Anil came. Nathan made two demands: a doctor, and a transfer to a room with its own WC.

An hour later, the boy returned. 'Forty-rupee room all full. Telephoning to doctor is tomorrow.'

'No, now. You must telephone him *now*. Today.'

'Yes, to-day. But he cannot coming before tomorrow. Wery busy man.'

'I am very sick.'

'Yes, sick.' Anil grinned. 'Doctor tomorrow. No problem.'

'I'm going to Delhi tomorrow. I have to leave here by twelve, so the doctor must come early. First thing in the morning. D'you understand?'

Anil wagged his head. 'Doctor tomorrow, no problem.'

'Here.'

The boy accepted the money.

Nathan stole a bucket from a storeroom on the landing. A metal pail, pitted with rust but intact. He carried it to his room, part-filled it with water and stood it in the corner, beneath the open window.

3. A Representative in Automotive Components

Morning diluted the shadows, exposing the contents of the pail – the unmistakeable colour. Nathan lifted the bucket on to the window ledge, tilting it towards the light, and studied the red until it could not be disputed. Even allowing for the container, the smell was ferrous: raw liver, menstruation, nose bleed. He set the bucket back down. Wiped his palms on his T-shirt. Jesus. Okay, what he had to do was get help because, what was it? It was only 6am, but he needed the doctor right away. He inhaled. If he could make it as far as the landing and shout down the stairwell... his bowels contracted. The bucket supported his weight once more, its rim etching deeper into welts of raised flesh. Five minutes, ten. Sweat speckled the floor between his feet.

In the night, he had dreamed of a policewoman calling at his parents' house with news of his death: mother, sobbing on the sofa; father, correcting the WPC's pronunciation of Jodhpur. He'd smiled in his sleep, storing his father's remark for the German. Give her a laugh. Make her like him. But she'd been there too, drinking tea with his parents, wanting to know where he was, where the goods were, threatening them; but they refused to betray him. All the while, Nathan – invisible, inaudible – screamed at them to tell her, to take her up to his boyhood bedroom, with its blu-tacked bands and footballers, and for *fuck's sake* show her the fucking hiding place.

The next time he woke to garish sunlight. There was a power cut. The fan must have been idle for some time because Nathan lay wreathed in moist sheets. Coming to. Watching the zigzag of flies in the corner of the room. What time was it? Five past ten. *Fuck*. He convinced himself Anil had fetched the doctor and gone away again, unable to obtain a response. He sat up, then stood, then let himself out, not bothering to lock the door or even close it. As he edged along the balcony, he had to shield his eyes against the reflective glare of the floor, the walls, the windows; making sure not to look down into the plaza, humming with dust and traffic, four storeys below.

Step. Step. Step.

If he focused on the floor directly in front of his feet,

concentrating, making each step his sole objective, then the next one and the next, he would reach the lobby eventually. And when they saw him, the state of him, they would have to help.

Step, step.

Nathan made the mistake of raising his head, trying to judge the distance to the landing. There was only sky. Blue smog-hazy sky. And the sky rearranged itself in a rude swoop, an arc, a blur of bright wide blueness that blacked into nothing.

A face loomed over him: moustache, small mole on the bridge of the nose, yellowish filaments in the whites of the eyes. A brown face.

'Are you the doctor?'

The face frowned, amended its angle. 'In actual fact, I am a representative in automotive components.'

'Where's Anil?'

'Excuse me?'

'The boy. The room attendant.' He tried to sit up, but a hand eased him back down onto the softness of a pillow. 'He–'

'Please, you need to rest,' said the face.

Nathan's breath came in rasps, fractured by coughing fits. His head throbbed. There was an alteration in him, in his skin, and it took a moment to identify towelling where there had been thin, damp cotton. He was wearing a bathrobe.

'Where are my clothes?'

'There are clean clothes when you are ready.' A hand indicated a chair where a pair of shorts and a striped T-shirt Nathan recognised as his own were laid out.

'Where did you –'

'I took the liberty of bringing them for you.'

'You went into my room?'

'Ah, you see, but you defecated all over mine.' A smile. 'So perhaps that makes us even?'

Nathan noticed the room, now. Much like his own as far

as he could see, only bigger, and the curtains were patterned with flowers. It smelled of aftershave. He shut his eyes, opening them again at the resumption of the voice.

'You fell outside my door. *Into* my door, in actual fact. I'm afraid your head is bleeding.'

There was a spasm in his gut. This time he would not be deterred – pushing, pleading; the hands that restrained him became his support, helping him from the bed and on to his feet. *Please, just here.* Nathan saw a partition with a doorway leading to a toilet and shower stall. The hands guided him. They held him while he squatted, confident arms hooped under his in a bear hug redolent of stale tobacco, spices and hair oil. That astringent scent of shaving lotion. When Nathan had finished, he fumbled with the tap, the scoop, the logistics of cleaning himself; then the hands other than his own took charge again: sluicing the water, a palm wiping him with efficient strokes before using a towel – gentler, now – to rub him dry. Nathan's eyes filled.

'Please, you are sick. There is no reason to be disgusted with yourself.'

The man was still at the bedside. He had changed. Instead of a vest, he wore a white short-sleeved shirt with a collar, a tie and gold-framed glasses. The distinctive red-and-white markings of a pack of Marlboro showed through the fabric of his breast pocket. He was smoking. Nathan watched his host's hands, the manicured nails and tufts of silky black hair on the back of each finger; hands that had cleaned him.

'By the by, my name is Venkat.'

Nathan said his own name.

'Do you object?' Venkat said. 'At home, I am not permitted to smoke.'

'How long have I been asleep?'

'A few minutes.'

'What time is it?'

The other man inspected his watch. 'Precisely eleven o'clock.'

'*Jesus.*'

'Don't worry, the doctor is coming. I have made the necessary arrangements.'

'I have a train to catch. To Delhi.'

Venkat shook his head. 'In actual fact, you are not in a suitable condition to travel from one side of this room to the other. So I think Delhi is a little ambitious.'

Nathan went to lift himself.

'Please, rest. Unfortunately I have business affairs to attend to, but I shall wait with you until the doctor arrives, if that is agreeable.'

'How soon will he be here?'

The man smiled, tilting his head to expel smoke towards the ceiling. 'In this country, things occur when they occur. Not before. But not afterwards, either.'

The abortive attempt to leave, the inability even to dress himself without fainting for a second time... with these failures came the fact, so stark in its irreversibility: the train had departed without him. He wouldn't reach Delhi that night, wouldn't keep his appointment with the German. He had collected the goods but would not fulfil his *obligation* to deliver them. That was the finality of it. Nathan, his face smeared with tears and spit and snot, became a small boy for a moment.

Venkat offered him a handkerchief. 'Perhaps, in a few days, you will be well enough to resume your travels.'

A traveller. That's all he was to this man. A young Western tourist who'd been taken ill while backpacking around India. Nathan wiped his eyes, nose, mouth with the handkerchief. The weeping was spent almost as soon as it had started. He tugged the borrowed bathrobe close about him, his body depleted and insubstantial. If there was strength, it existed elsewhere; he was not the one with the strength now. Even his host – slightly built, gentle – looked capable of snapping Nathan's limbs one by one, like chicken bones.

'My room, I've left my valuables in there. Money, passport, and that.'

'It is locked. And I have brought your valuables.' He indicated the bedside table, where Nathan's room key rested on his money-belt, with its familiar sweat stains. His iPod was there, too, and so was his phone. Not that he'd been able to obtain a signal at any point in Rajasthan.

'You have no camera? I could not find one.'

The thought of Venkat searching his room sent a bolt of panic through him. 'No,' Nathan said, trying to stay casual. 'Well, yeah, but it got stolen in Jaisalmer.'

'Ah, Jaisalmer. I have never visited.'

Nathan briefly described the ancient fort's labyrinthine alleyways, the four-day camel trek, the drought that had littered carrion – cows, goats, dogs – in the villages of the desert margins. The screech of fighter jets patrolling the border with Pakistan which, one night, was as close to the camp as Jaisalmer itself. He did not talk of the transaction, completed by moonlight in those bleached wastes while the others in the party slept in their bivouacs, oblivious.

'You should go there some time.'

His host frowned. 'In actual fact, in the more primitive regions of my country the demand is not so great for automotive components.'

His task had been simple: collect the goods, then deliver them. In the appointed place, at the appointed time. *Be there, Nathan. Do not be late. Do not fail to deliver.* If he let her down, it would cause her to let down other people. She couldn't allow that.

Nathan handed back the snaps of Venkat's family, their names and ages exchanged for details of his own relations back in England. The business card was Nathan's to keep, his host's home address – in Delhi – written on the reverse.

Venkat zipped it inside Nathan's money-belt. 'There, inside your passport, for safekeeping.' He slipped the photos back in his own wallet. 'Before you leave India you might care to visit, and my wife will cook for you?'

Now that he knew of the years Venkat had spent in Birmingham, learning his trade, Nathan could detect the trace of an accent. *Villa Park, the Bull Ring, the NEC, Edgbaston.* On the other man's lips, these intended intimacies only made Nathan's homeland more inaccessible than ever.

He faked tiredness. Then the feigned sleep became real; when he awoke again it was dusk and the incense of a smouldering mosquito-coil perfumed the air.

'Where's the doctor?'

'The doctor is coming.'

4. The Arrival of the Doctor

These sleeps were the best: the dreamy, drifting, anaesthetised loops of waking and semi-waking and deep slumber where pain was imaginary, light as foam and diffused on the breeze of each exhalation. In these hallucinogenic sleeps, the stink of himself, the wetness between and beneath, his legs: none of it mattered. The goods, the delivery: none of it mattered. He saw the German's face on the wall, hologrammed, telling him it was all right. She could not reach him because he had transcended punishment and forgiveness; if he could only pass to the land beyond sleep he would be safe from her forever. But Venkat's moustache, the mole on the nose, the gold-framed glasses, his voice... These were the threads that snagged him in the real.

'Let me go.'

Cold water splashed his face. 'Please, you must drink.'

'No, I have to meet someone.'

'Here.' The water was in his mouth now. 'Try to swallow.'

At least he still had the packages, hidden away in his room. She couldn't accuse him of doing a runner with them or cutting a deal with someone else. There *was* no-one else. Only her. Surely being late wasn't as bad as not delivering at all?

Venkat was trying to make him drink again, warning of dehydration.

In the hours that may have been night, Nathan had flown an imaginary plane in the dark, its drone – the mantra of a bee swarm – always on the point of stalling, of cutting out and plunging the aircraft down into the spiralling black. Nathan, willing it. But, in daylight, with water being spilled and words coaxing him to drink, the engine noise persisted in the erratic gyrations of a ceiling fan in a strange room.

'You must've missed your business appointments.'

'In actual fact, these matters were not so important.'

'Where did you sleep?'

'Here, in the chair.'

'Thank you, Venkat. I'm sorry.'

'Please. There is nothing to be sorry for.'

Voices were using Hindi. He had the embarrassed sense of having just spoken out loud in his sleep. Any amount of time might have elapsed since the last spell of lucidity, the last conversation. Was he participating in this one? No. Drowsy as he was, the words – their furtive tone – turned his head towards the source of the sound. There was Venkat, framed in a rectangle of bright light with the silhouetted figure of a boy. Anil. In the instant before the door closed, Venkat held Nathan's gaze.

'What? What's happened?'

What? What's happened?

But he was alone, now, with no-one to hear him. The digits on the phone were blurred. Three o'clock? Four? It didn't seem possible, but this was the afternoon of his second day in Venkat's bedroom. Something was wrong. The guy's not-quite-overheard exchange with Anil had left a taste, a lingering unease. When Nathan moved, his bowels immediately emptied into the towel that had been swaddled about him as a makeshift incontinence pad.

Where was Venkat? Nathan spoke the name, but received only the resonance of his own voice on blank walls. He called out. The exertion triggered a sequence of harsh coughs that left him breathless. The doctor. That would be it. Not trusting the boy, Venkat must've gone to find the doctor and bring him here personally.

'Venkat? Are you there?'

No answer.

Fuel tanks, radiators and exhaust systems for the motor vehicle repair and maintenance sector. That was his area of special responsibility.

He had promised to wait with Nathan until the doctor arrived. He'd promised.

The mosquitoes were biting: ankles, ears, knuckles – wherever the veins were vulnerable. If the coils and matches were within reach, maybe he could light one. He must've been sleeping again because the light had seeped from cream to grey. Nathan had no idea how long he'd been alone, but the apprehension of waking up unattended was easing now that he understood the reason. Anil had come – when *was* that? Today, yes, this afternoon – to report that the doctor had been delayed. And Venkat was out there now, in the city, explaining the urgency of the circumstances.

Hadn't he lit a coil? He thought he had.

Soon there would be footsteps on the balcony. Nathan could easily imagine Venkat's voice, the ushering in of the doctor and, momentarily, he became euphoric at the thought of receiving treatment. Of being well again. He considered what to say, after the handshakes and introductions. *Doctor, I'd be grateful if you could prescribe something to stop me shitting blood in my friend's bed.* He rehearsed the phrase aloud, over and over, making himself laugh so long his ribs hurt.

What was Venkat's wife called? S, something. *Sunita.* Sunita, he had to be sure to memorise that. What about the children? One boy, two girls. Or was it the other way round? He couldn't, for the life of him, recall their names.

He was thirsty. Where was the water?

That sleep felt like a long one, although the room wasn't much darker than when he'd drifted off. Still no Venkat. Yet his absence was a kind of presence. Nathan liked that notion. Thinking about it, this room was full of absentees: Venkat, Anil, the German, the doctor, the old woman who cleaned the rooms and swept the floors, the men who would track him down and levy the penalty for his failure to deliver. If the levy didn't happen here, it would occur somewhere, sometime. But he was here, now. In a hotel in Jodhpur. Bedridden. He was going nowhere.

'I'm going nowhere, pal.'

The water stood on the bedside table. If he rolled his head to one side, he could see the bottle. The upper half was empty, just moisture pearling the inside of the plastic. The water in the bottom half looked cloudy. He reached out, but his arm was too heavy, his fingers too incoherent.

Footsteps. They passed by the window and he heard the unlocking of a door, followed by noises in the neighbouring room. The turning on of a tap.

Nathan manoeuvred himself so that he could lever his shoulders off the bed, lifting his head and propping himself on his elbows. After a brief rest, he managed to push again with his heels. He was almost sitting up now, the wooden headboard hard against his spine and his skull lolling back into the wall.

Why was Venkat taking so long to bring the doctor?

Nathan regulated his breathing, counting each inhalation

until the urge to vomit receded. Now, the water. He looked at the bottle on the bedside table. The money-belt was still there, along with his room key, phone, iPod; even on the cusp of nightfall he could distinguish their forms. But there was something else, now. Black, glossy, irregularly shaped. Like a cat, crouched there or curled asleep, its long tail dangling over the edge of the table. He allowed his vision to adjust to the failing light.

Not a cat.

Strips of black sticky tape and polythene, all tangled up in a ball.

It was a moment before he was confident enough to free a hand without fear of toppling off the bed. There. He dragged the mess on to his lap, knocking the bottle to the floor, where the water inside continued to slop back and forth after the bottle itself had come to rest. Although he realised already that it was pointless, Nathan began unpicking the tape, trying to free the parcels. Only they were no longer parcels, as such – just empty polythene bags, punctured and ripped and crumpled, bearing just the faintest powdery traces to show what they'd once contained. Even, then, with all the entangled tape and scraps of polythene in his hands, he couldn't accept it for what it was – couldn't quite let go of the hope that it was just another hallucination.

He recalled the expression on Venkat's face in the doorway, as he'd met Nathan's gaze, and understood it for what it was now.

Looking around the darkening room, he saw that the clothes rail beyond the foot of the bed was strung with empty hangers and the suitcase no longer stood in the corner. The bathrobe, which had been washed and draped to dry over the back of the chair – that was missing too. If he could've made it to the bathroom, he was sure the wash bag would have gone from the ledge above the basin. It was possible that he'd find more traces there, in the basin or around the toilet – unless

Venkat had sluiced them all away.

Nathan set the straggle of tape and packaging down on the bed and wiped his hands again and sat for a few minutes, resting against the headboard.

He didn't need to, but he looked anyway – taking his money-belt from the bedside table and clumsily unzipping the compartment containing his passport. He opened it, thumbing through the pages for Venkat's business card. It wasn't there.

The room was pitch-dark. Nathan lay on his back, listening to the muted sounds of the night. Somewhere in the hotel, music was playing on a radio; in the street, way below, people shouted above the buzz of traffic. In the room, there was only the tock-tock of the fan. He sniffed the dispersed air for the scent of aftershave or Marlboro cigarettes, but the room's pervasive odour was of himself. His body felt unnaturally light, held in place on the bed by the weight of the sheet; he pictured himself, a chalk-figure in the black. He closed his eyes. Waited for sleep. For dreams. For the footsteps, the voices, the knock on the door that would announce the arrival of the doctor.

Here's a Little Baby,
One, Two, Three

SHE DELIVERED US HERSELF, at home – no midwife, no birth-partner. *Like a bird hatching its young*, she says, as if it was the most natural thing imaginable. It meant no-one could take us away from her. Connor was the first. Then me, Beth, about ten minutes later. *Twins*, our mother thought, assuming it was over. Then Aidan turned us into triplets.

Three babies, one mother, no father. Our family.

Aidan was the runt. Sorry, but he was. From the moment of his birth – in the womb, as well, I suppose – he was the smallest, weakest, frailest of the three of us. It was as though he'd been assembled from the scraps left over after our mother had made Connor and me. Not that my share amounted to much; but I'd fared better than my little brother. Let me say that I loved Aidan; please don't think I didn't. From the beginning, his was the hand mine grasped whenever the three of us were laid side by side on the big quilted playmat. His was the ear or cheek I would suckle at, mistaking his tiny head for a breast. When he was hungry, which he always was, I'd let him suck my fingers for want of anything else.

'It was like the two of you was joined,' Mother has told me. *Conjoined*, she means. 'If you wouldn't sleep, all I had to do was put Aidan in the cot with you and you'd snuggle up and be off in no time.'

I realise that makes our mother sound normal. She wasn't, isn't. But we had no notion of it at the time. She was our only example of motherhood.

The only person we ever saw, for that matter.

Her first problem was this: three babies to feed and only two breasts. (She tried bottle-feeding but none of us would take it, not even Connor.) Connor was the second problem. From the start, our older brother was brawnier and noisier than Aidan and me put together; he cried the loudest and longest, squirmed about the most, flapped his arms and legs more vigorously, clamped on tighter and sucked harder and for longer. If there was any milk going, Connor's clamouring ensured he had the first helping. Once he was latched on, there was no shifting him till he'd drunk his fill, and then some. So our mother would position him on one side while Aidan and I took turns to feed on the other. Even then, Connor wriggled and fussed, jerking his chubby limbs at whichever one of us happened to be there. It was as though he wanted to knock us off the other breast in case he needed it for himself. So Mother says. Of course, he was just a baby; a fidgety, boisterous, hungry baby. There was no malice in it.

I loved Connor, too, regardless of what you might think.

In those early weeks, the physical disparity between us became increasingly apparent. Connor, with all the milk he guzzled, grew bigger, fatter and stronger at a startling rate; he'd been a kilogram heavier than me at birth, according to the bathroom scales, but by the time we were six months old he weighed almost twice as much as I did. Meanwhile, Aidan became more runt-like, dependent on the dregs of milk that remained after I'd had my turn. Sometimes, our mother tells me, she would doze off with Connor at one breast and me at the other, and wake up to find she'd been drained dry, with Aidan grizzling and unfed in his cot.

Things were no better after we were weaned. Mother would sit us in our highchairs in the kitchen and spoonfeed us puréed fruit or vegetable straight from the jar.

'Soon as I buckled the three of you in your chairs, Connor would kick off.'

I've heard this tale so often, I picture it as if it's a memory: my big brother, red-faced with rage, mouth wide open, howling for food – thumping the tray and rocking back and forth so hard the highchair jolted a few centimetres across the floor towards our mother as she reached into the food cupboard. Against his demands for attention, my own cries and Aidan's feeble mewling barely registered.

She fed Connor first, always. One of those little jars after another: parsnip, butternut squash, spinach, carrot, apple, banana... he didn't care, as long as it kept coming. Four or five helpings at least. Once each jar was finished, Connor set up his commotion again as our mother unscrewed the lid of the next. *Mine*, his wails said. *Mine, mine, mine*. Often there'd be only one jar left for me and Aidan to share. Most of it went to me.

There isn't a day when I don't feel bad about that.

None of this amounted to deliberate neglect on Mother's part; she only did what she thought was right. 'Baby will tell you when he's hungry,' her parenting book said. 'Baby will tell you when he's had enough to eat.' So she fed her babies according to whichever of us told her they were hungriest.

Anyone else would have seen straight away that Aidan was dangerously underweight. But no-one visited and Mother never took us out of the flat. Apart from any neighbours who heard us crying, nobody knew we existed. Nobody who mattered, anyway. As for our mother, she saw us as she had always seen us, and which she took to be the natural order of things:

'Connor was the big one, you were the middle one,' she says, always with a wistful smile, 'and Aidan was the little shrimp.'

As far as she can remember, we were about seven months old when Aidan went to sleep and wouldn't wake up. For a few days, she continued as before: lifting us from our cots in the morning, changing our nappies, dressing us, placing us in our highchairs, feeding us, laying us on the playmat, and so on. Last thing in the evening, she bathed us and put us in our sleep-suits and lay us back in our cots. Day after day, Aidan 'slept' through all of this, entirely unresponsive. Floppy to begin with, then stiff, then limp again. At feeding time – once Connor and I had finished – our mother held Aidan's head up while she pushed spoonfuls of mush between his lips, only for it to dribble back out of his mouth.

Naturally, we were oblivious, Connor and I. However motionless and silent, our little brother was still there, alongside us, as he'd always been. I dread to think what state he must have been in as the days went by. But, on the playmat, so I'm told, I would snuggle up to him as usual and offer him my fingers to suck.

Then, one day, Aidan was no longer with us. Mother must have taken him somewhere during the night because, the following morning, there were only two babies to be raised from their cots, to have their nappies changed, to be dressed and carried into the kitchen for breakfast. We were twins again, me and Connor.

'What did you do with him?' I have asked our mother, many times.

She remembers so much, but she tells me she can't remember that.

We were too little to miss him, she says. But I miss him now.

Connor learned to roll over on to his front and could sit upright without support and shuffle around on his bottom. He was soon crawling, too. Such was his strength that, when he set up his kerfuffle at meal times, he could almost tip the highchair over altogether. He demanded more food than ever. Mother gave it to him. And while all of what remained would come to me, now, there was less and less of it. He outgrew the highchair and had to be switched to a booster seat at meal times. Often, our mother says, he grabbed the spoon off her and tried to feed himself. But the gloop went everywhere and this sent him into a rage that didn't let up until she prised the spoon from his fist and took over again. Rusks and fingers of buttered toast, he managed by himself – cramming pieces into his mouth as if they were plastic blocks to be forced through the holes of a shape-sorter.

I found my brother's antics hilarious, apparently. At the kitchen table, I couldn't take my eyes off him as he ate. On the living-room floor, no matter how many toys he snatched from me, I would pick up another and hold it out for him to grab – giggling with delight as he did so. Once I was able to crawl, I'd follow Connor wherever he went. Not that I could keep up with him for long. Or that he wanted me to. But however cross he became, however fast he crawled off, however roughly he shoved or batted me away, I dragged myself after him, undeterred.

'You used to wear yourselves out,' Mother says.

I picture myself sprawled face-down on the carpet, panting like a stranded fish on a river bank; Connor, glowering at me from the far side of the room, flushed and furious.

The more active we became, the more calories we needed. There was never enough to eat, though – the benefit payments didn't stretch far, especially as Mother couldn't claim for three babies that didn't officially exist. Of the food she did manage to provide, my brother commandeered an ever-increasing proportion for himself.

More, his bellowing seemed to say, now. *More, more, more.*

Every few days, Mother left us at home by ourselves while she went to the supermarket. I don't know whether her absence distressed us; I suspect we would've learned to stop crying once we realised she wasn't there to respond. Nor would it have taken us long to understand that she would return sooner or later with more things for us to eat. We must've figured out when she was about to reappear in that doorway, too. Whether her footsteps alerted us, or the rustle of the shopping bags as she set them down on the step, or the click of a key in the lock, it's hard to be sure; but our mother would open that door to find us scurrying towards it.

'Your brother used to charge at me on all fours, like a chimp!' is how she describes it. 'I'm hardly through the door and he's under my feet and tugging at them bags.'

Me? I'd usually be playing catch-up along the hallway, or sitting by the door to the living room, sobbing my little heart out. As if it was a race and I hated to lose. Alternatively, it's quite conceivable that I was upset because Connor had given me 'a bump', to use another of Mother's phrases – that, in his determination to reach her (or the food) first, my brother had barged me out of the way. Just as he had tried to jostle me, or Aidan, off the breast. Just as he'd whack me whenever I trailed him around the flat. There's no evidence, of course. By the time our mother let herself in, the deed would already be done. But I can easily imagine him flapping those meaty elbows, shoving me into the living-room doorframe, or dumping me against the skirting board, or into the radiator in that narrow hall.

At eight months old, I still fitted into the clothes I'd been wearing at half that age; if anything, they were loose on me. Having learned to crawl, I'd now lost the knack, or the will, or the strength to do much more than squirm around like a worm. When I sat up, I toppled over. My neck muscles no longer supported the weight of my head.

I wasn't the middle one anymore, I was the little one. The runt.

You might have expected our mother to learn from what had happened to Aidan and make sure to feed me enough. She didn't. To this day, though, she believes events took their natural course, regardless of any action, or inaction, on her part.

'Sweetheart, you just wasn't as hungry as Connor,' she says, matter-of-factly.

Baby will tell you when he's hungry.

Connor told her sure enough. First to the door, first to Mother, first to the bags of food. Pulling out jars and tins and packets, right there on the doormat, holding them up for her to open, or bashing them against her legs. *Howling*, the whole time.

'Honestly, Beth, you never heard the like of it. And his *face*.'

The gaping O of his mouth.

She'd have to break open a packet and shove a rusk or biscuit in his hand, just to distract him while she hauled the rest of the shopping into the kitchen. If I followed *her*, Connor would barrel along the hallway and knock me out of the way. If I approached *him*, on the front mat, hoping for a share of whatever she'd given him, my brother held the food out of my reach with one hand and smacked me in the face with the other.

'The pair of you. I swear, you was enough to try the patience of a saint.'

She didn't have to put up with this *squabbling*, as she refers to it, for much longer. I'd never been able to compete for attention, or food; now, in my increasingly weak state, I must have given up trying. As Mother remembers it, I became less and less mobile. At meal times, I sat impassively, half-asleep or staring into space, while Connor kept up his usual clamour. Whatever scraps came my way seemed to puzzle me, as if I couldn't remember what food was or what to do with it. At play time, I'd simply lie there on the floor, not attempting to crawl – uninterested in the toys, or in pursuing my brother as he careered around the living room. When our mother

141

returned from her shopping trips, Connor was the only one heading down the hallway to intercept her. She would find me where she'd left me.

My brother had 'won'. But that didn't diminish his determination to go on winning.

By now he was sturdy enough to pull himself up to standing and would cruise around the flat, holding on to furniture, door frames, walls. He even managed to walk a few steps unaided before flumping on to his bum. Anyone seeing us for the first time might have assumed he was older than me by months, not minutes; that I wasn't his twin but his little baby sister.

I was dying. My body was shutting down, along with my will to live. Slowly but surely, I was starving to death.

To our mother's mind, this was just the way of things: babies weakened and died, as Aidan had done; or they grew stronger and survived, as Connor was doing. I'd turned out to be another weak one. It might take a matter of days or weeks but, when the time came, she would have to smuggle me outside under cover of darkness and dispose of me, as she had disposed of Aidan.

'But you're still here!' she laughs, clapping her hands, as though applauding me for making it into adulthood. Or perhaps she's applauding herself. 'My little miracle.'

If anyone deserves applause, it's Connor. He was the one who saved my life.

My brother was no longer content to wait for the sounds of our mother returning from the supermarket before charging up the hallway. Now that he was able to stand, he would position himself by the front door the moment she left and remain there until she came back. She discovered this when, one time, she made it to the front gate before realising she'd left her purse behind. As she turned back, she saw the top of Connor's head in the frosted-glass panel of the door's upper half. He must've been holding on to the handle because, when

Mother twisted the key and pressed down, his head disappeared from view and she heard the familiar whumph of a nappy-padded bottom hitting the floor. From then on, she had to take care whenever she let herself back into the flat in case she clunked him.

'It was a job to get in at all, sometimes,' she says.

What did I do, while our mother was shopping and Connor stood guard at the front door? Lay on my back in the living room, I guess, like a discarded rag-doll among the scattered toys – gazing up at the ceiling, waggling my tiny fists and feet in the air, arching my back, trying and failing to roll over. Or craning my neck to see where my big brother had gone. Not even this much, probably. No doubt I could hear him out there in the hallway. Knowing Connor, he wouldn't have waited patiently for Mother's return. Before long, he would've started his bellowing; he would've been thumping the door with one hand, tugging and rattling the handle with the other – his hunger, his indignation, his rage, mounting with each minute she was gone. Beating out his mantra: *Feedmefeedmefeedmefeedme.*

Then came the day when, as she set off for the supermarket, our mother must have forgotten to lock the front door behind her.

On her return, she found it wide open and Connor gone.

I like to think that she searched for him.

That she dropped the bags of food and hurried into the flat, dashing from room to room, checking every cupboard and hidey-hole, heart thudding, breath burning her throat. *Where is he?* I imagine her asking me, pointlessly. *Where's your brother, Beth?* I like to think she ran outside and looked for him in the street – peering into gardens, behind walls and hedges, under parked cars, shouting his name all the while. Weeping. Knocking on doors, stopping passers-by: *Have you seen Connor? Have you seen my little boy?*

I've asked her, and she says she must have done all of these things.

But it's just as possible – perhaps more likely – that Mother arrives home to an open door and is momentarily confused by it. *Oh, the door's normally shut.* She puts the shopping bags down, as usual, and reaches into her coat pocket for her key, before realising that – *silly* – she doesn't need it. She carries the bags inside, pushes the door closed and locks it. *There, the door's shut now.* But, in the flat, she finds one baby instead of two. This confuses her again. Just as Aidan confused her during those few days when he wouldn't wake up.

'Where's the other one?' she asks me, in this version of events.

Of course, I don't answer. I just lie there gazing up at her.

Mother remembers the food at this point and the purpose of her shopping trip: *Go out; buy food for baby; bring food home; feed baby.*

I am baby now.

'Come on, you,' she says, lifting me up and taking me through to the kitchen. She straps me into my highchair. She fetches the bags and unpacks all of the jars and packets and tins. Finally, she opens one of them.

'You hungry?' she asks, in her 'mummy' voice.

I tell her that I am.

Connor was discovered a couple of days later.

It seems he'd found his way to the passage along the side of the building and followed it into the rear courtyard, where he had tumbled down the stone steps that led to a boarded-up basement flat. The pathologist's report said he died from a fractured skull. By the time one of the binmen spotted him, my brother had been partially eaten by scavengers; dogs, foxes, rats. Crows. His eyes and tongue had been pecked out.

I've read the newspaper reports. I wish I hadn't.

Whenever I think of Connor, now, it's the picture of him

at the foot of those steps that pushes all of the others away.

The police conducted door-to-door inquiries in an attempt to discover who the little boy belonged to. Whether one of the neighbours pointed the police in our direction, or our address was simply next on the list, I don't know. Whatever, the police came calling. They saw the way things were with our mother, with me.

She was taken away and I was taken into care.

That was thirty-one years ago.

In a few months' time, I shall have a baby of my own. I have just told Mother the news that she is to be a grandma. I think she understands. She must do because, after a moment, she asks if she can place her hand on my bump *to feel him wriggling around in there*. I let her, even though the baby is still too small for any of that.

'You used to get the hiccups when you were in my tummy,' she says.

I return her smile.

When she says 'you', I have no idea if she means me, or all three of us.

We talk about other things, as best we can. But she leaves her hand on my belly the whole time, only removing it when one of the care assistants pops her head round the door to let us know it's time for Mother's tea.

The Beckhams are in Betty's

I heard the news while I was at the dental surgery. The hygienist had looped the paper bib around my neck and was reclining the back of my chair when her phone pinged.

'Excuse me,' she said, picking up the phone from the side and studying the screen. 'It's from my daughter.'

'You're okay,' I told her.

When someone asks to be excused, you excuse them. I do, anyway. But it's not okay for a dental hygienist to interrupt the treatment of a patient to read a personal message, is it? Not that she'd begun treating me at that point, in fairness, or even completed the lowering of the chair to horizontal.

'Oh my *God*,' she said, still looking at the phone. 'The Beckhams are in Betty's.'

One of those phrases which makes perfect sense, linguistically, but, at the same time, is incomprehensible.

'The Beckhams?' I asked, although I might as easily have said 'Betty's?'

'My daughter works there,' the hygienist replied, as if I had indeed said 'Betty's?' 'She says The Beckhams just came in.'

'Both of them?'

'The kids as well, apparently. The whole family.'

The Beckhams, in Betty's. It was something to think about. I found myself trying to recall the names of the children, not altogether sure how many they had. Brooklyn, that was one. Romeo. Was there a third, a fourth? My wife would've known. Names, ages, everything. She would've been much better suited to that conversation than I was. The hygienist seemed not to mind, though; I suspected she was simply pleased to have someone – anyone – to share the news with.

'They're up for the grondy-pa.'

It took me a second to realise she'd said 'Grand Depart'. (I should have explained, this was back in 2014, when Yorkshire hosted the first stage of the Tour de France.)

'Are they?'

But the hygienist was preoccupied with thumbing a message – a reply to her daughter, I assumed. Oddly, she had pulled her mask into position over the lower half of her face, as if the phone might be contaminated.

The next day, on the news, there he would be – David – launching the race. At that moment, though, he was a couple of hundred metres away – in Betty's, with Victoria and an indeterminate number of children. I could well imagine the ripple of collective awareness among the other customers as The Beckhams entered the café. I had been in there a few weeks earlier, when Alan Bennett was at a neighbouring table. He'd angled himself towards the wall, reading a newspaper that partially concealed him from prying eyes. Only a few of us registered him, I think. Of course, we made a conspicuous effort not to let him know we'd noticed him. But, with all due respect, Alan Bennett isn't David Beckham. He isn't Victoria Beckham, for that matter. Alan Bennett, in Betty's, is not a surprise of seismic proportions – indeed, you could almost believe Betty's had been designed with him in mind.

'I know he's a bit young for me,' the hygienist said, laughing, 'but that is one man I would *not* kick out of bed.'

She was referring to David Beckham, of course, not Alan Bennett. 'Hah,' I said. 'No. Quite.'

She gave me a curious look. Placing her phone down again, she rolled her chair back towards mine. 'Sorry about that.' She completed the reclining process and passed me a pair of protective glasses. 'But it's not every day The Beckhams are in town, is it?'

I came close to saying 'No. Quite,' again. Instead, I put on the glasses and opened my mouth in anticipation of being asked to do so.

'Any problems since I last saw you?'

'No. Nothing to report.'

'Gum bleeds?'

'No.' *Only when I eat pineapple*, I didn't tell her.

'Good. Good.' She wheeled herself closer still and adjusted the anglepoise lamp, momentarily blinding me. 'Right, let's have a look, shall we?'

I opened my mouth again, wider.

As she set to work, I remembered something I'd seen on the way to the surgery – seemingly inconsequential at the time. Walking along The Grove, cutting it fine for my appointment, I had passed two sharply dressed figures heading in the opposite direction. Sauntering side by side, as if they had time to kill and nothing much to kill it with. They both wore nothing but black. The woman: dark-blonde ponytail, slim, smart jacket and skirt, heels; the man: built like a rugby player, goatee, earpiece, suited and booted. The PA and the bodyguard? They were smiling, chatting, relaxed with each other and within themselves. Like they mattered. Like the street was theirs. I'm not sure how much of this had struck me as I passed them, or whether it only occurred to me afterwards, while I was with the hygienist.

All the same, I mentioned them to her when she paused the clean-and-polish for me to rinse my mouth. It wasn't the same as having seen The Beckhams themselves but it came close. Although only the upper portion of her face was visible above the mask, she looked pleased with this additional information. *One of my patients saw their personal assistant and bodyguard wandering around town*, she would tell people. Her daughter. I dabbed my lips and lay back down.

'Where d'you think they're staying?' she asked.

'The Travelodge in Keighley, I expect.'

She laughed. 'I reckon The Devonshire. Open wide for me.'

Just then, his last-minute goal against Greece came to mind: the bend-it-like-Beckham free-kick that clinched our place in the World Cup Finals. Or the European Championships? Whichever it was, the opposition couldn't have been more apt – David Beckham was heroic, in that moment. Adonis-like. Herculean.

A fine-looking man, my wife once called him. He is. He's a fine-looking man.

'I wouldn't want to be that famous,' the hygienist said. 'You couldn't go anywhere without being gawped at, could you?'

Given the nature of her job, it seemed probable that patients were continually gawping at her. Naturally, I didn't say so; not least because she was digging between my molars with a stainless-steel pick. All I could offer was a grunt of assent.

'And the kids,' she added. 'It can't be a normal life for them.' I managed another grunt. After a moment, the hygienist, said, 'She's on food prep. She isn't actually serving them.' Her daughter, I gathered. 'You *couldn't*, could you? *I* couldn't.' She laughed. 'My hands would be shaking so much I'd spill tea all over him.'

What if he was your patient?, I was unable to ask. If she had to insert her surgical-gloved fingers between David Beckham's lips, would her hands shake then? They weren't shaking, with me. But if I have one thing in common with Alan Bennett, it's the fact that I'm not David Beckham. It goes without saying that I'm not Alan Bennett, either.

'It's a bit spongy,' the hygienist said, prodding my gum. 'Just where the bridge is. Make sure you floss properly round there.'

I grunted 'yes'. But her phone pinged again and she was already turning away.

I can't account for my behaviour after I left the dental surgery. I could say that I acted out of character; but I did what I did

– so, surely, it must have been *in* character? Not typical or predictable, perhaps, but self-evidently within the range of behaviour of which I am capable.

I should be careful not to over-dramatise. We're not talking a Mark Chapman-John Lennon scenario. It isn't that kind of story.

Here's what happened.

From the surgery, I walked back along The Grove, heading homewards. (My route would take me past Betty's, so it's not as if I went out of my way.) Over the years, I've had a handful of encounters with celebrities on The Grove. By 'encounters', I mean 'sightings'. Richard Whiteley, the former Countdown presenter – I saw him two or three times; one of the cast of Emmerdale (I forget his name); a woman who might have been the cyclist, Lizzie Armitstead; the actor who played Neville Longbottom in the Harry Potter films. This last one doesn't really count because he was there to switch on Ilkley's Christmas lights. Hundreds of us 'sighted' him that evening. Can't recall his name, either. But the point is that all of these people are, or were, known to live in the area, so it wasn't especially startling to see them in town. Mild surprise probably covers it: the frisson of registering the fact that a face you're used to seeing on a screen is right there in front of you, in the flesh. Close enough to touch. Close enough for you to speak to them. Not that I ever did either of those things.

I mention all of this only by way of establishing that I am not usually fazed by a brush with celebrity. That afternoon, however, a knot of tension formed in my chest. My breathing became shallower and more rapid. My palms prickled with sweat.

The Beckhams. In Betty's.

I decided to go into the café.

As I approached, I saw that two expensive-looking vehicles were parked outside. Had they been there earlier, when I'd passed by en route to my hygienist appointment? I hadn't noticed them. And yet they must have been there, if the PA and bodyguard had already been strolling along the street by that time. One was a big, black SUV, the other a sleek Mercedes, also black. I think it was a Merc; I'm not great on makes of car. The vehicles sparkled in the sunlight as if they were glazed with gold. I'm being fanciful, here. All I'm trying to say is that, even in an affluent town like Ilkley, they looked several cuts above the cars which are typically parked along The Grove.

The Beckhams' vehicles, then.

The broad, cherry-tree lined pavement bustled, as it always did, with shoppers, tourists, people going about their business. I had no sense that any of them were aware of The Beckhams' proximity. The realisation that I was the possessor of secret knowledge tightened the knot in my chest. To them, it was a regular weekday afternoon and Betty's was just another shop front, as unremarkable as The Grove Bookshop, WHSmith, Johnsons Cleaners or Oxfam. To them, I was just another anonymous pedestrian. No paparazzi, I noticed; although it was surely only a matter of time before the café's other customers scattered the breadcrumb trail of tweets and instagram posts that would lure the first of the paps. Or, at the very least, a photographer from the *Ilkley Gazette*.

There were no other customers, though. Betty's was closed.

That is, the door was locked. Beyond the glass frontage, the lights were off and the bakery section was deserted – display cases of fancy breads and cakes, with no-one to sell or buy them. The short corridor leading to the café at the rear, and where a queue can usually be seen, was similarly unlit and empty. The two tables visible beyond the 'Please wait here to be seated' sign were laid but unoccupied. While I peered in, an older couple tried the door, too, before walking away, expressing puzzlement that Betty's should be shut at that time of day.

I tested the door again. Damn. How could the place be...

The penny dropped: Betty's must have been closed specially for The Beckhams. So that they could take afternoon tea in private, ungawped at, untweeted, unphotographed. The Beckhams obviously had the entire café to themselves.

I turned this realisation over. Had they paid for this exclusivity, compensating Betty's for the loss of business? Or, when the call came from The Beckhams' people (that pony-tailed PA, perhaps), had the manager been only too delighted – *honoured* – to accommodate them? Then there were the logistics: ensuring that all of the customers who'd been in there earlier in the afternoon had left by The Beckhams' scheduled arrival time. Keeping it quiet from staff beforehand so that no warning of the visit leaked to the media. Standing down most of the waiting and kitchen staff for the period – an hour? – when only one table was in use.

'Is it *closed*?' a voice said, behind me.

I turned round, stepping back from the window and trying not to appear flustered. Or furtive. 'Fraid so.'

'Bugger.'

The woman looked thirty-ish, vaguely Mediterranean, although her accent sounded local. Posh Yorkshire. Her shoulders were swathed in a pale-green pashmina and her dark hair had escaped in places from the assorted clips and pins that kept it out of her face. Green eyes, to match the pashmina.

'There's no sign,' she said.

'No. But the door's definitely locked.'

She gave a small sigh of impatience. 'I only wanted a walnut loaf,' she said, partially raising a hessian shopping bag for me to see, as if to authenticate her remark. Or as if I had some influence over the situation that might enable her to buy the walnut loaf after all. More likely, she was merely expressing her annoyance out loud, rather than for my benefit. I just happened to be there. In the same way that I'd happened to be in the hygienist's chair when she needed someone with whom to share the news of The Beckhams.

'The Beckhams are in there,' I told the woman. That got her attention.

'What?' A frown etched a double speech-mark between her Frieda Kahlo eyebrows.

'It's why Betty's is shut. The Beckhams are having tea in the café.'

The speech-mark deepened. 'Posh and Becks?'

'And the kids. Brooklyn, Romeo... the whole family.'

'Seriously? The Beckhams are – '

'– in Betty's, yes.' I nodded at the unlit interior. 'They've got the café to themselves.'

'No!' The frown had given way to a tentative smile. A sceptical one. *Okay, this is the point when you tell me it's a wind-up,* her face said.

My mouth was dry and my pulse whooshed in my ears, but I feigned a nonchalant matter-of-factness. 'Yeah, I had a tip-off.'

'What d'you mean, a tip-off?'

'I'm a journalist. Freelance.' I indicated the small rucksack on my shoulder, allowing her to imagine it contained a notebook, camera and such like. In fact, it held a folder of paperwork relating to my job as an independent financial adviser, which I'd brought along in case the hygienist's appointments were running behind schedule.

To this day, I don't know why I told that woman I was a reporter. *It just came out,* is the only explanation I can offer. But, of course, nothing just comes out.

Once I'd said it, I was committed. 'They're up here for the Grand Depart,' I added.

'Oh, okay.' A verifiable fact for her to latch on to. She nodded, smiled a little more fully, ineffectually tucking a stray lock of hair behind one ear.

She was looking at me quite differently, by then. We'd moved beyond walnut loaf. To be honest, I was disappointed by how easily she'd been taken in. How easily I'd impressed her. Curiously, she'd accepted (the lie) that I was a journalist far more readily than she'd believed (the truth) that The Beckhams were in Betty's.

'They're staying at The Devonshire, apparently,' I said, substituting 'apparently' at the last moment for 'according to my sources'. Better to be implicit than to show off.

The woman nodded again. *The Devonshire. Of course.*

As I had done, she leaned close to the window and peered in, her breath misting the glass. 'So, they're in there,' she said. A statement, not a question, her tone underscored with a silent 'wow'. She might've been a teenage groupie hanging around the stage door, hoping for a selfie with a singer whose posters covered her bedroom walls.

She turned to me again, her point of contact with The Beckhams, who were otherwise impossibly, tantalisingly, out of reach beyond that locked door. 'Will they speak to you?'

I shrugged. 'David'll be fine but Victoria can be a bit prickly.'

Where was this *coming* from?

She looked satisfied with that answer, though. 'Yes, I can believe that.' She flicked another glance through the window. At the empty queuing area, I imagined, or at those unoccupied tables in the only visible part of the café. 'I was never into the Spice Girls,' she said. 'But, if I was, she'd have been my fifth favourite.'

We both laughed.

'Mind you, I never used to be all that keen on him, either,' she went on.

'No?'

'Sure, he was always a *pretty boy*, but...' She searched my face, as if the right words might be inscribed there. 'He has grown into himself as he's got older, hasn't he?'

'I know what you mean,' I said, not entirely certain that I did.

We shared a brief, contemplative silence. Then, her eyes all glittery, she asked, 'Is this what you do, then? Celebrities. Your speciality, I mean.'

'Oh. No. No, no – the celebs just buy me time to work on the more serious stuff.' I gestured at Betty's. 'A few pictures, couple of quotes – that's a month's earnings right there.'

'So, which other *slebs* have you done?'

'I, er – recently? – well, there was Alan Bennett. He was in Betty's as well.'

The woman wrinkled her nose. 'Can't imagine you got a month's earnings for *him*.'

'No. Quite.'

She studied me for a moment. One end of her pashmina had come loose and dangled down her front so that she looked as if she was wearing a large pale-green question mark. She swung it back over her shoulder and, turning towards Betty's window once more, said,

'How exciting, to be standing this close to a *scoop*.'

After she'd gone, the nature of my deception settled on me. I was 12 years old again, telling Marian Fogden I'd met Donny Osmond during a family holiday in America – showing her his signature in my autograph book, which I'd written myself, left-handed, after practising on a sheet of paper. The holiday was in Sussex.

Pathetic. Utterly pathetic.

There was still time to catch up with the woman – I could see her weaving through the pedestrians at the end of The Grove – and apologise for pretending to be something I wasn't. Naturally, I didn't. Having impressed her, I couldn't bear the thought of the look in her eyes when she understood what I'd done. And what it said about me.

Marian Fogden. I didn't know I remembered her name, until I remembered it. We'd learned the lyrics to *Puppy Love* and used to sing it together on the roundabout at Addington

Park, lying on our backs and gazing up at the revolving sky. Back then, I dreamed of meeting Donny Osmond. Dreams so vivid I'd wake up convinced that we'd met for real: in the sweet shop, on the bus, at the library. One night, absolutely certain that he was playing hide-and-seek in my wardrobe, I got up to look. He wasn't in there, needless to say. Another time, I dreamed I'd been knocked down by a stretch-limousine (white, tinted windows) and Donny stepped out to check I was okay. When he saw my injured leg, he ordered the chauffeur to drive me to the Osmonds' mansion, where I spent several weeks recuperating. Oddly, the Donny in each dream had no recollection of having met me in the other dreams.

I loved Donny Osmond. More than I loved Marian Fogden. I loved him so much it hurt my ribs, it hurt me to swallow. I could make myself cry just thinking about him.

I moved away from the door before anyone else tried to enter and asked me whether the café was closed.

What I didn't do was continue on home.

The important thing, to my mind – the only thing that mattered – was to confirm for myself that The Beckhams were in Betty's. As if that might in some way redeem me for the lie I'd told the pashmina woman; or what the motivation was, I couldn't altogether be sure. It's fair to say I'd taken leave of my senses by then. That, even as I tried to rationalise my behaviour, I was acting irrationally.

The Beckhams. I had to lay eyes on them.

It was easy enough to *visualise* them, clustered around a table – two tables pushed together, perhaps, depending on the number of children. Anyway, there they all are, with plates of crustless sandwiches, fingers of cinnamon toast, a Fat Rascal studded with glacé cherries and almonds, a tiered cake-stand laden with small pastel-coloured fancies arranged on paper doilies. Victoria pouring tea. The flowery scent of Earl Grey or a smoky Lapsang Souchong.

'Not at the table,' she says, and Brooklyn (Romeo?) rolls his eyes as he pockets the phone (or iPad) he's been browsing. Yes, Brooklyn. Romeo is colouring in; they give out children's activity sheets and tubs of crayons at Betty's. Unless Romeo is the eldest?

David helps the little one (is there a little one?), who has an arm tangled in the strap of her – let's say it's a girl – booster seat. Or high chair. He picks up a toy she has dropped and she gurgles and flaps her tiny feet as he hands it back to her. Then she flings it away for Daddy to retrieve again. It's summer, David is wearing a lemon-coloured, short-sleeved shirt that accentuates his tan. The little one is fascinated by the tattoos on Daddy's arms and loves nothing more than to trace the patterns with her fingertips. One of the waitresses is fascinated by the tattoos as well. She hovers nearby, but not too near. She fetches the extra napkins which Victoria has requested to mop up the Diet Coke that spilled when Romeo jogged the table, colouring in too vigorously.

Surrounding them, an arena of deserted tables. Silence. The ghosts of a hundred absent customers. David looks around a little anxiously, as if half-expecting unwanted attention, then relaxes again at the sight of all those unoccupied chairs. He licks butter (cake crumbs?) from the tip of his thumb and laughs at something Victoria says.

No good. Any of it. All I had was a locked door with no sign of life beyond.

I walked the short distance to WHSmith and cut down the service road that runs behind the parade of shops along The Grove. One option would have been to stay put in front of Betty's and wait for them to leave. I'd have had my proof, then. But loitering outside the café held no appeal. In a small town like Ilkley, where I've lived for many years, it would be quite feasible for someone I knew to spot me standing there and I'd have to explain myself. Besides, there was no telling how long The Beckhams might take over their afternoon tea. By tracking round to the back, I could peer in through Betty's rear windows – directly into the café – and see them for myself.

What I'd forgotten was that the service area is several metres below the level of The Grove, with a row of retail units tucked in beneath the ones above. There, Betty's windows were well above head height.

I stood and stared up at the leaded panes, with their panels of stained glass, as if there'd been a mistake. Or as if the building's structure was an Escher-like optical illusion and that, if I waited long enough, the anomaly would rectify itself. I'm being fanciful again. What I was doing, in fact, was taking a moment to register my stupidity. *Of course* the rear windows were too high to see in.

Scouting round for solutions, my gaze alighted on the recycling bins beside the public toilets. Just long enough for me to dismiss the idea as ridiculous, it crossed my mind to clamber on to one of them. Instead, I retreated to the adjoining pay-and-display car park. Now that I was no longer directly beneath Betty's, the perspective was better. I could see the tables arranged along the café's windows. All of which were unoccupied. Naturally. Why would The Beckhams go to the trouble of reserving the entire café to allow them to take tea in private, then ask to be seated next to a window? As I withdrew further, more of the interior came into view. By this point, however, I was so far away that the tables and chairs were reduced to shadowy shapes, too indistinct for me to tell whether anyone was sitting there, let alone identify those people. I watched for a while, hoping to discern signs of movement or activity: a waitress crossing the room, the turn of a head, the lifting of a cup. Anything.

There was nothing.

A car horn jolted me from my distraction. I was standing in the path of a red Peugeot whose driver was reversing out of a parking space. Or possibly a Renault. I can't be sure the vehicle was a French make, to be honest, but the point is I moved out of the way, raising a hand in apology. For some reason, I wondered if the driver might be the pashmina woman. It wasn't. The guy looked barely out of his teens. Purple-tinted sunglasses.

'In La-la land, there, pal,' he said, unimpressed, through his lowered window as he swung past. He steered one-handed, the other arm resting on the sill.

'Yeah, sorry about that.'

He shook his head, muttering, 'Fucking no-mark,' as he pulled away, a sudden blast of music from the sound system cutting off any reply I might've made. I'm aware that it's an improbable coincidence, but he wore a yellow T-shirt and his arm was heavily tattooed.

No-mark. Nice one. I watched his car till it was lost from view.

Then, after a final, lingering look at Betty's rear windows, I retraced my steps across the car park and up the service road beside WHSmith. Back to Option 1, then: Wait outside the front of the café for The Beckhams to emerge, however long that took.

As they came out, David would look around, I expected, making eye-contact with passers-by, dispensing smiles, nods. Victoria wouldn't; just the pouty scowl. They'd each be holding hands with, or carrying, one or more of the children. I'd be among the onlookers. I would receive one of David's smiles. If the mood took me, and the logistics were favourable, I'd reach out for a handshake. He might even let me have one, you never knew. Then they'd be across that broad pavement, where the bodyguard and PA would already be in position by the open doors of the SUV. With The Beckhams secure, the bodyguard and PA would climb into the Mercedes, if it was a Mercedes, and the convoy would sweep away. All over so quickly, the bystanders would swap glances, exchange remarks, to confirm that their eyes hadn't deceived them: that they really had just witnessed The Beckhams leaving Betty's.

None of that happened.

As I turned along The Grove, I spotted the gaping spaces where the two black cars had been parked. I saw, as well, that Betty's had re-opened.

Withen

EVERYONE FILED OUT OF the chapel to gather by the wreaths, which were arranged in front of the stand bearing Dad's name, sharpening the air with their scent. We stood in the September sunshine, too warm in our formal clothes. People said what a lovely service it had been. My sister-in-law, Tanya, told me how much she'd liked my speech.

'You did Don proud.'

The note cards were still in my fist, bent into a tube and damp with sweat. I thanked her. Slipped the cards into the pocket of my suit jacket. Suzy caught my eye through the crowd of mourners and mouthed, *You okay?* I nodded. She was with Mam, stooping to retrieve the cellophane-wrapped messages and reading them out to her. The dutiful daughter-in-law. Not that my mother would have had more than the vaguest idea who Suzy was.

Rich nudged my elbow. 'What the fuck's he doing here?' he said, under his breath.

I looked where he was looking. A figure stood at the top of the steps that climbed a grass embankment above the chapel. The thick brows, the great dome of his head. Uncle Peter. Thirty years older than the last time I'd set eyes on him, but unmistakeable.

It should have fallen to me to take charge of the situation. But ever since the two of us were big enough to fight, the age difference between me and Rich had seemed notional. I was the kid brother, I just happened to have been born first. That's how it had been when I was a boy; I felt no different now, aged fifty-three.

'We just pretend we haven't seen him?' Rich said, as if I'd suggested exactly that.

Tanya must have cottoned on that something was wrong. 'Who is it?'

'Dad's brother,' I told her.

She hadn't met Uncle Peter but it was clear she knew all about him. She laid a hand on my brother's sleeve. 'Don't make a scene, Rich. Not today, not here.'

Richard freed his arm and, before we could stop him, made his way over to the steps.

1984

When the footage came on, Chinese subtitles scrolling down one side of the screen, I didn't realise what I was watching at first. Becca sat beside me on the bed. We were drinking beer and swapping stories from our day, half an eye on the news. The TV was parked on a chest of drawers across the room. In an 8th-floor bedsit of a 17-storey block in Tsim Sha Tsui, huddled among the high-rises of Kowloon, the violence played out through a fuzz of interference:

Missiles arcing down on the police lines.

Close-up of a cop, blood staining his blond sideburn bright red.

Long-haired guy in a T-shirt and jeans, aiming a kung-fu kick.

Police in riot gear, scattering people across a scrubby, dusty field.

Mounted cops in formation, riding – cantering – right at the men as they fled.

It was only when I heard 'Orgreave' that I finally caught

on. I gestured at the TV with my beer bottle. 'Fucking hell, that's just a few miles from where my folks live.'

We'd arrived in Hong Kong four weeks earlier. You could pick up work as an English tutor – no qualifications required, or teaching experience; they just wanted native English speakers for one-to-one conversation. By the day of Orgreave, I'd been travelling for nine months: the US, Canada, Australia, Papua New Guinea, Indonesia. I celebrated my 23rd birthday in the March, in a bar in Singapore with a few others from the backpackers' hostel.

That week, in the UK, the miners' strike had started.

'Your dad's out,' Mam announced, when I phoned so that she could wish me a happy birthday. 'Rich as well, and Uncle Peter.' I'd read about Corton Wood and the other pits in the *Straits Times*, so I wasn't surprised the walkouts had spread to Withen Main. It was more than that, though. 'Arthur's called out the whole country,' Mam said.

She always referred to Scargill by his first name, as if he was a friend of the family.

'Should I come home?'

'What good would that do, love?'

That remark still niggled me later, in the bar. I drank too much, too quickly, and wound up in an argument with the only other Brit. Branwell. Twenty, on a gap year.

'The miners are already paid heaps, aren't they?'

'They're not striking for more money.'

'Why then?' What other reason *could* there be?, his expression said.

'To save the pits from closing. To save their jobs, their families.'

'How does that work?' Branwell laughed through his nose. 'They close a pit by going on strike to stop the pit from closing. Genius.'

'If the government shuts a mine,' I said, 'it might as well shut down the whole community. But you wouldn't know about that, would you, living in Hampshire.'

He studied me through the cigarette smoke. 'I mean, who'd even want to work down a coal mine anyway?'

'My dad. My brother. My uncle. Most of the lads I were at school with.' *Were.* I hadn't said 'were' instead of 'was' in about five years.

'Not you, though. And remind me, Matt, where is it you live now?'

I took a slug of beer to stop myself from calling him a *Tory wanker* right there in front of everyone. We'd become a spectator sport, me and Branwell.

The table jolted, spilling someone's drink, as I stood up and headed for the toilets.

Branwell hit one nail on the head. I'd been backpacking since September but I'd been away for years. Since going to journalism college in Harlow. There was an identical course at Sheffield, a bus ride from Withen, but I'd wanted to be near London to pick up shifts on the nationals. That's why, when I graduated, I took a job on the *South London Press* instead of applying to the papers back home. Dad had asked if I was trying to tell them something. It was his way of letting me know I would be missed, while also reminding me where I was from. Rich had put it more bluntly. *Matt's too clever for Withen, Dad.* Three and a bit years I worked at the *SLP*, sharing a rented house in Gipsy Hill with a vegan motorcycle courier who said *Ay oop lad* every time I entered a room.

After I'd finished skulking in the toilets, I went to buy another drink, delaying the moment when I'd have to rejoin the others.

'You're very cute when you're angry.'

It was one of the Kiwis, standing beside me at the counter. She'd only arrived at the hostel that morning. Blonde, freckly, pretty. She looked like she enjoyed making mischief.

'Sorry about that,' I said.

'About what?'

'Souring the mood. Pooping the party.'

'It's your party, birthday boy.'

'And I'll cry if I want to.'

'Besides, that guy's a total dick.' She pronounced it 'duck'.

I laughed. Sade was playing. *Shady*, Mam called her; not *Sharday*. 'What's that?' I asked, pointing to what looked like a dried-out chilli on a cord round the Kiwi girl's throat.

'A Maori aphrodisiac charm. Makes me irresistible to men.'

'Does it work?'

She laughed and gave me a thump on the arm.

'Can I get you a drink?' I asked.

'At *last*, he gets the whole point of the conversation. I'm Becca, by the way.'

We travelled together after that night. Malaysia, Thailand, Burma. Now there we were in Kowloon, watching Orgreave.

'Is that the pit where your lot work?'

'No. And Orgreave's not a pit, it's a coking plant.' I explained about turning coal into coke for use in steel-making. 'The miners are trying to blockade it.'

'Would any of your folks have been there today?'

On the TV, a car had been set alight. 'Rich, maybe,' I said. 'Not Dad or Uncle Peter, I wouldn't have thought. They're a bit old for scrapping with the plods.'

The footage ended. The bulletin cut to the studio and a No. 3 typhoon warning.

2014

Once they'd finished talking, Uncle Peter turned away and walked stiffly along the path that led to the car park. My brother rejoined us, tugging his tie loose.

'Said he'd come to pay his *respects*.' Rich ran a hand over the lower half of his face, as if checking whether he needed a shave. In fact, his skin was perfectly smooth, still pink in places with razor burn. 'I told him he were about thirty year too fucking late for that.'

I glanced back up at the path but Uncle Peter was already lost from view.

My brother and his wife joined Mam in the funeral car, along with their kids. It eased away so quietly you wouldn't have known the engine was running. I told Suzy about Rich confronting Uncle Peter. If she had an opinion about that, she kept it to herself. Laura and Ben stood with us, both on their phones, messaging. We headed away from the chapel along the wooded path, the last of the mourners. This year's leaves had yet to fall but last autumn's still lay on the ground in places, dry as paper underfoot.

'Thanks for looking after Mam back there,' I said.

'She kept asking where your dad was.'

'What did you say?'

'That Don had probably snuck off somewhere for a smoke.' When I didn't respond, Suzy added, 'I didn't know what to say for the best. I mean –'

'No, I'd have most likely said the same. Anyway, he would've, wouldn't he? If Dad was here, he'd have been having a crafty fag.' I checked that Laura and Ben weren't lagging too far behind. 'Remember the first time you came home? He was so stressed at meeting you he got through about thirty Woodbines that afternoon. I've never known him pronounce so many aitches.'

'They kept calling you *Matthew*.'

'Did they?' I let out a laugh. 'I'd forgotten that.'

'Actually,' Suzy said, 'I think they were as nervous of you as they were of me. In case they let you down in front of your new London girlfriend.'

That evening, we'd gone down to the Welfare with Mam and Dad for a drink and to introduce Suzy to my brother and Tanya, who was his fiancée then. Rich had just finished a shift and was telling us about a runaway tub which had nearly wiped someone out.

'The work must be *so* dangerous,' Suzy said. 'I can't imagine how you guys do it.'

There was a pause. I saw Rich and Dad exchange glances; they could decide to feel patronised by this poshly-spoken southerner, or they could let it go.

I cut in. 'Tell Suzy about your accident, Dad.'

Dad looked at me. He saw right away what I was doing. He wasn't one for talking all that much, since he'd developed his stammer – but he told her the story. Told it the way he always used to, for people hearing it for the first time, punctuated with sips from his pint.

'This w-were a few year ago,' he began. 'I were cu-cu-cutting wi' me mate, Ralph, when there were this almighty gruh-great crack. D-dint 'ave time to dive out way or owt. Buried up to me chest, like. It were right quiet at first and me lamp 'ad gone out, so it were puh-puh-pitch black. Then I heard Danny Rudge go, "No, Ralph – Don's gone." Well, I th-th-thought they were just going to leave me there. So I managed to get me 'ands fuh-free – there were these two w-w-wooden props holding most of weight off me – and I'm banging about and shoutin', "I'm all reet!" And then Ralph and Der-Danny come scrambling over this gu-gu-great slurry heap and start pulling me out.'

'Were you hurt?' Suzy asked. She'd been hanging on every word.

'Me-me legs w-w-were stuck, see.' He fell quiet, staring at his beer.

'Tell her, Dad,' Rich said. I loved him for saying that. For playing along.

Dad shook his head, blinked away the moistness in his eyes. 'You tell 'er, son.'

Rich pointed at Dad's legs. 'He lost them both,' he told Suzy.

Silence around the table.

'My *God*, I had no *idea*,' Suzy said, her own eyes welling up. 'You lost *both* your legs?' she asked Dad.

After a moment, he said, 'Nuh-nuh-nuh-not me legs, no. Me boots.'

'Your *boots*?'

'Aye, brand new they w-w-were. I paid a flamin' fortune for them boots.'

We all fell about laughing. When Suzy called us a *bunch of bastards*, we laughed harder still – and she was laughing loudest of all.

We emerged from the shade of the trees into the car park, bright as an over-exposed photograph. Suzy aimed the fob at our VW and popped the locks. It was only as I shrugged off my suit jacket and opened the front passenger door that I spotted him, sitting on a bench in the small water-garden below the parking area.

From the back, it might've been Dad. A plume of cigarette smoke feathered in the air above his bald head. I remembered my uncle as broad, stocky, barrel-chested – like one of the wrestlers on World of Sport. Mick McManus. Although Rich reckoned he looked more like the baddie in Thunderbirds. We used to pretend to hypnotise each other behind his back whenever he, Aunt Sylvia and our cousins came round. Sitting there, smoking, he appeared stooped and round-shouldered. Shrunken.

1984

On the way back from the international telephone exchange, I spotted one of the COAL NOT DOLE stickers on the subway. Rich had sent several sheets of them, *post restante*, and Becca and I stuck them wherever we could. I've no idea what the local people made of them. The few of my students who knew of the strike were bemused by what they'd seen on TV.

'Why police not have water guns?' one had asked me. Leon. All of our students chose Anglicised names for themselves, in addition to their Chinese ones. Cindy, Peggy, Irene, Flora, Charles, Marvin. Mercedes, in one case.

'Cannon,' I corrected Leon. 'Water *cannon*.'

'Yes, water cans and crying gas and rubber bullet. Why England police not have?' He sounded puzzled but also indignant, as if some natural law had been breached.

Kowloon-side, Becca was waiting for me in the café in the basement of our building, sitting at one of the Formica-topped tables, a fat teapot and two small cups set out. Steam rose off her tea; when she saw me, she smiled and began pouring mine. The place was full. We were the only non-Chinese.

'I've ordered congee,' she said, as I sat down opposite her. 'That okay?'

I would have preferred toast and eggs but I said, 'Yeah, that's good.'

Billy Joel was playing on the radio. Uptown Girl. The Hong Kong stations had run a continuous loop of his songs since we'd arrived. When they weren't playing Two Tribes.

'How're things at home?' Her tone was bright; it was just a regular phone call – the weekly check-in with my folks – so she had no reason to suppose anything was wrong. Then, as she set the teapot back down, she must've taken a proper look at my face. 'Matt?'

I was so tremulous I couldn't believe the cups didn't rattle as I placed my palms on the table. The sour fumes from the tea made my eyes water. 'Dad's... in hospital.'

'Your *dad*? No.' Her chin puckered. 'What... I mean, how is he? Is he okay?'

'Yeah, the hospitals are full of people who are okay.' I don't know where that came from, or what she'd done to deserve it. I waved a hand as if to erase the words. 'Sorry.'

The waitress appeared. She was about ten years old, in

blue dungarees and wearing a Beatles haircut. She set down the bowls and plates: thick rice-and-fish porridge and tubes of spongy bread. In our first week in Hong Kong, after months of Southeast Asian food, we ate McDonald's every day. More recently, we'd been conditioning ourselves for mainland China.

The girl told us to *enjoy*, looking delighted to have spoken this one word of English.

After she'd gone, I said, 'There was a swelling on the brain, but it's come down.' I couldn't meet Becca's gaze. 'Mam thinks he might be out by the weekend.'

I drew two pairs of chopsticks from the dispenser and handed one to her, still in its paper sheath. It was noisy in the café: clatter, conversation, music.

'What happened?' she asked.

'He went to Orgreave with Rich. My uncle as well.' I popped my chopsticks from their wrapper. 'Dad got separated from the other two.' I took a breath. 'Apparently, the cop hit him three times – once to knock him down, then two more whacks while he was on the ground. Two that Dad can remember, anyway.'

'Jesus.'

'They're going to charge him.'

'Good. Too bloody right.'

'Not the cop, my dad.'

'*No.*'

'They're just waiting for the doctors to say he's well enough to be questioned.'

'Charge him with what?'

'With whatever they like. Just *being* there is enough.'

As we picked at the food, I recounted what Mam had said. How things had become too lairy for Dad's liking on the field and how he and Uncle Peter had retreated to the village, *out of harm's way*. How the rest of the pickets were eventually forced back there, too – across the railway line, or over the bridge –

and how the police had gone after them, hunting them down. Dad *was in wrong place at wrong time*, as Mam put it.

I couldn't understand what he was doing at Orgreave in the first place. Rich was the flying picket. He went wherever he was needed – down to Nottinghamshire, if he could sneak past the roadblocks. Dad stuck closer to home, at Withen Main, standing outside the pit where he'd worked since he was sixteen. 'It's only a token,' he'd said, one time, when Mam passed him the phone. 'It's a hundred per cent, here. Other morning, a pigeon flew over gates and me and your uncle shouted *Scab!* for sake of summat to shout "scab" at. Even the coppers laughed.' Dad was a veteran of the '72 and '74 strikes. He was in his thirties, back then; at 48, he no longer needed to prove himself on the lines. Picketing was just something you did. *Tha gets less macho wi' age.* He pronounced it 'macko'. Rich was 21. Him and the other young lads were going for it, according to Dad. *Like bloody football hooligans, some of 'em.*

I pushed the bowl away. For a moment I thought I might be sick. I saw Becca sneak a glance at the clock on the wall. Eight-forty. Our first tutorials were at nine.

'What are you going to do?' she asked.

'I'll go in. I can't just not turn up.'

'I didn't mean that.'

The Longest Time came on the radio. 'Billy fucking Joel,' I muttered, but she paid no notice. She was waiting for me to answer her question. The actual question. I'd never known Becca look at me like that – as if she didn't recognise me.

'I don't know,' I said.

'Yes you do, you just can't say it to me.'

2014

'Now then,' I said, sitting down beside him. After thirty years, 'Hello Uncle Peter' would've sounded too juvenile, and calling him plain 'Peter' didn't seem appropriate either.

He must have heard me approach because he showed no sign of being startled; a brief glance, that was all, as if to check which one of us it was.

'Matt,' he said, with a slight nod.

The bench faced a perfectly oval pond fringed with ornamental grasses, encircled by a brick path and a margin of neatly laid pebbles. Like a water feature in a Japanese garden. For a moment I was put in mind of Becca; the faintest of blasts from the past.

'You're just about the last person I expected to see today,' I said.

'Aye, Rich said much the same back there. Only wi' more effin and jeffin.'

'I can't believe my brother swore. You sure it was him?'

Uncle Peter let out something that might have been a laugh. 'Anyhow, I don't need telling twice, Matt. So, I'll finish this,' he raised the cigarette, 'and be on me way.'

I gazed out across the valley, the sweep of pasture and woodland.

'There are worse spots to sit,' I said.

The last time we'd seen one another, he was several years younger than I am now, his face looming at a bedroom window of his darkened house. Below, in the garden, I'd stood with my brother. We'd already thrown two half-bricks through the downstairs windows but Rich insisted we stay so that our uncle saw who'd done it.

I pointed to a sapling close to the pond, a plaque planted in the soil at its base and blue-and-white ribbons fluttering from the spindly trunk. 'Wednesday fan, d'you think?'

Uncle Peter nodded. 'Well, his suffering is over now.' I couldn't help smiling. He'd always been the joker of the family. 'I can see their ground from my house,' he added.

'You're in Sheffield these days?'

'Walkley Bank, aye.' He paused. 'You still follow Leeds?'

174

'Not really. I watch them when they're playing in London, that's all.'

He took another draw on his cigarette. 'Never knew how you could support that lot.'

'Broke Dad's heart, me being Leeds.'

Every other Saturday, we'd stand on the Lowfields terrace – arriving an hour before kick-off, so I could bag a place at the front of the middle tier. Dad would watch the game with his little radio pressed to his ear, to find out how Rotherham were getting on. That radio – one of its successors, anyway, held together by two rubber bands – was in the bedside cabinet at the hospital when Rich and I cleared out his personal effects.

'When he was ill,' I said, 'even quite near the end, he always got me to read out the football stories from the paper, if I was visiting.'

I would feed him, too: spooning yoghurt into his mouth, or tinned peaches cut up small for him to swallow. I shaved him. Trimmed his toenails. When Dad soiled himself, I washed him and replaced his incontinence pad. I didn't tell Uncle Peter any of this.

'Cancer, wor it?' he asked.

'Leukaemia.'

'It were bowel, wi' your aunt.'

'Aunt Sylvia died?'

'Two year ago.'

We'd reached this point, where people died – *family* – and we didn't know, or even know where they lived, or anything about their lives any more.

'How did you hear about Dad?'

'I still get *Advertiser* sent over. Saw it in funeral notices.' Uncle Peter had finished his cigarette. He pinched the tip between his thumb and middle finger, as Dad used to, and slipped the stub in his jacket pocket. 'I weren't going to come,' he said. 'But...' he let the sentence trail off with a shrug.

I finished it for him. 'He was your brother.'

'Aye, he was. When all's said and done, we were brothers.'

He stood up, with difficulty, one hand holding the back of the bench for support. *New hip*, he explained. Looking in the direction of the car park, he asked, 'That your missus?'

I stood as well. 'Yeah, Suzy. Those are our kids in the back: Ben and Laura.'

Their faces were towards us, hologrammed by the sunlight on the glass.

That night in the winter of 1984, our uncle hadn't come downstairs; he'd remained at his bedroom window, motionless – watching us, watching him – until Rich and I turned away, let ourselves out of his garden and headed off down the silent street.

'Will you come back?' I said. 'To the wake.'

'I don't think that's a good idea, do you?'

'I'm asking you. I'd like you to be there.'

Uncle Peter turned towards me. 'You don't half have a look of him, you know.'

'I was thinking the same about you.'

After a moment, he said, 'What about Rich? The old lags from pit?' He still held on to the bench, standing at an awkward angle, as if one leg was longer than the other. A sheen of sweat had formed in the greyish stubble above his top lip. 'What about your mother?'

'It's Dad's funeral,' I said. 'Not theirs.'

1984

It was Saturday before I could get a flight out of Hong Kong; Sunday, when I stepped off the bus at Withen. Dad had been discharged the day before. He was lying in bed with the curtains shut when Mam took me up. The light gave him headaches, she explained. The room smelled of stale sweat and the lemon barley water which stood in a jug on the bedside table.

'Matt's here, love.'

But Dad was dozing. I set the dressing-table stool beside the bed and watched him sleep while Mam went downstairs to make a brew. In the gloom, the gauze patch on his head might have been a scrap of paper that had blown in through the window and landed there. Dad looked as if he'd aged about ten years in the ten months since I'd last seen him.

He woke before Mam reappeared, rolling his head to one side and blinking at me as if he suspected I might be a figment of his imagination.

'Hello Dad.'

'W-wuh-wuh-what're you doing here?'

'Nice to see you, too.'

'You should've st-stayed in Hong Kong.'

'That whack on the head has made you less grumpy, then.'

'I told her you'd do this.' Mam, he meant. 'Told her nuh-nuh-not to say owt to you.'

Mam was in the doorway, carrying a tray of tea and biscuits. The logo on one of the mugs read: *NUM – Support the Miners*. 'Who's "her"?' she said. 'The cat's mother?'

Dad pushed himself up into a sitting position while I repositioned the pillows at his back. 'How long have you had the ponytail?' he asked.

'Couple of months,' I said.

'Don't start on him, Don. He's just flown half-way round world to see you.'

When Rich came in later, he gave the ponytail a flick. 'You Matt's girlfriend?'

'Very funny,' I said.

'Hey, Dad, what d'you reckon?' My brother half-turned me towards the bed. 'Is it just me, or does Matt look like the back end of a police horse?'

The ponytail had been Becca's idea. My hair was already collar length when I left England and I'd decided not to cut it the whole time I was away.

'You know what would really suit you?' she said, trailing her fingers through my hair after the first time we'd made love.

So, by the time we left Singapore, I was a ponytailed man.

We'd been politely awkward with each other during my last three days in Kowloon; as if preparing for, or protecting ourselves from, the other's absence. We revised our plans: I would somehow scrape together enough cash to fly out and rejoin her, when Dad was fully recovered. If I couldn't, she'd travel to Europe anyway. To England.

I'd been home two weeks when I received a blue airmail envelope. It contained a long, lovely letter which ended with Becca saying she'd decided to go to Japan.

The editor at the *South London Press* agreed to rehire me as a features writer. I moved back down to London. Anything spare from my wages, I sent to Mam and Dad. The strike was four months old by then and Mam was the only one bringing any money into the house, from the little she earned as a school dinner lady and the part-time cleaning job she'd taken on. They'd sold the car, Rich's drum kit and hi-fi system, the bone-china crockery and walnut sideboard Mam had inherited from Gran. Most of their food came from donations to Withen Women Against Pit Closures, which the committee divvied up between the striking families.

When she wasn't working, or making sandwiches at the Welfare, or shaking a collection bucket in Rotherham for the WWAPC, Mam toured the country with some of the other women to give talks and raise funds. I'd even set up a visit to South London, to address the local trades council. To see her before a room full of strangers – nerveless, articulate, informed – was a revelation. At home, the sole woman in a house of opinionated men, she was usually more of an observer than a participant whenever politics cropped up. But there she was, at Lambeth Town Hall, bringing a hundred people to their feet in applause. I recorded every word for the piece we ran in the paper.

'Make no mistake, this dispute isn't just about coal mines, or the mining industry, or miners. It's about all of us. All of *you*. What we're witnessing is nowt less than a planned attack on the British working class and our communities. Mr. Ridley, Mr. MacGregor, Mrs. Thatcher – they hate us. And, if we let them, they will destroy us.'

When the clapping finally subsided...

'The prime minister didn't batter my husband at Orgreave. She didn't put him in hospital. You won't find her fingerprints on that truncheon.' Mam paused. 'But when I look at my husband – my Don – and see what he's become since that day, Mrs. Thatcher's shadow hangs over him as surely as if she were standing right there in the room.'

The police didn't charge Dad in the end. They might as well have banged him up in a cell, though, because he'd more or less imprisoned himself in his own home. He spent most of his waking hours watching television, filling the living room with cigarette smoke. He no longer picketed. Seldom left the house at all, except to sit in the back yard with the *Daily Mirror* or the *Rotherham Advertiser*, if the weather was fine.

The doctors couldn't tell if the speech impediment was physical or psychosomatic.

'He's lost confidence in himself,' Mam said, when I was home one weekend and we were alone in the kitchen. 'A cupboard door bangs and he jumps like he's been shot.'

'He looks as if he's lost weight,' I said.

'Well, he would do. There aren't many calories in Woodbines and PG Tips.'

I tried to piece together what happened to him at Orgreave. But Dad was reticent about it and Rich had become separated from him in the chaos and so didn't witness the incident. According to Uncle Peter, Dad was hiding behind an ice-cream van when he got hit.

'An *ice-cream* van?'

'Aye, *Rock on Tommy* it were called.' He, Aunt Sylvia and our cousins had come round for Sunday dinner because it was cheaper to use one oven than two. 'I'd gone on to Asda to buy some sarnies and left your dad queuing for 99s.'

'Blimey,' Rich said, 'you two aren't exactly Fidel Castro and Che fucking Guevera, are you?'

We all laughed around the table; even Mam, despite the language. Even Dad.

'When I headed back from supermarket,' Uncle Peter went on, 'the street were swarming wi' coppers, chasing our lads all over place. Running into folks' gardens and everywhere. You were already on ground by then, Don. This feller from Thurcroft had taken his T-shirt off and were using it to stop blood from where you'd been clobbered.'

'D'you remember any of that, Dad?' I asked.

'I remember p-payin' for 99s. But I don't remember gettin' any ch–chuh–change.'

The thing from that day that sticks in Dad's mind above all else is the vibration from the police horses' hooves as they cantered across the field. *You could feel it in your feet and right up your legs.* I've lost count of the times he's told me that in the years since.

In the film footage and photos which I've trawled through, I've only ever found one shot of my father at Orgreave. It's in a video clip of pickets rolling a tractor tyre down the slope towards the police lines. You can make out Dad, Uncle Peter and my brother in the background. Dad throws his head back, amused by something Uncle Peter says. They look happy, drenched in sunshine, shirtless in Rich's case – like three men on a works outing to the seaside. I've asked, but none of them can recall what my uncle said to make Dad laugh.

2014

'You'd never know it had been there, would you?' Uncle Peter said.

We were in his little green Corsa, following Suzy along the road that passed the industrial estate where Withen Main had once stood. The wheel from the winding gear had been installed like a piece of modern sculpture in a small park at the bottom of the high street but, otherwise, there was no trace of the colliery in the village. Even the air was fresh, these days, the once seemingly indelible acrid stench from the coke ovens long since dispersed.

'I remember Mam phoning me,' I said, 'the day they announced it was closing.'

I was on *The Guardian* by then. The features editor packed me off to Withen with a photographer to put together a colour piece, a *personal reflection* on the village where I'd grown up and the death of its coal mine. Eight hundred words.

'Never seen a site cleared so quick,' my uncle said.

'You came back in '92?' He had already been gone seven years by then.

'Just to see it one last time. Only it were nowt but a big wasteland wi' a JCB levelling it off.' He steered into a turn. 'Christ, when I think of the years I spent under there.'

'What did you do?' I asked. 'After you left.'

We were heading up the high street, with its pound shops and charity shops, betting offices and loan dealers. People were eating at tables on the pavement outside the chippy.

'Bit of labouring,' he said. 'Cab driving, this and that. Last few year, before I retired, I were a car park attendant at Sheffield Hallam Uni. *Professor of Parking*, my girls called me.' The gears crunched as he shifted up. 'How about you? You still on papers?'

'No, I'm a journalism lecturer, now. At Goldsmiths.'

'Funny how we both ended up working in Higher Education,' he said, and I laughed.

181

Then he asked if I was still *a union man*. I told him I was, for all the good it did, seeing as the management paid us little or no attention. 'Hardly anyone turns up to branch meetings, anyway,' I said. Me included, I might have added. 'We have a one-day strike, they dock us a day's pay, then we all carry on as if nothing had happened.'

Uncle Peter asked if Dad found work when the pit closed.

Not then, I tell him. For the next nine years Dad was on benefits, then – just as he hit retirement age – Asda took him on part-time: rounding up the trolleys, emptying the waste bins, tidying the delivery bay and recycling area, that sort of thing. It affected his pension but he was just glad to be doing something. It was apparent that Uncle Peter knew none of this.

By the time we followed Suzy into the restaurant car park, we'd gone quiet. His knuckles, misshapen by arthritis, were white where he gripped the steering wheel.

'Didn't this used to be The Kestrel?'

'It changed hands about ten years ago,' I said.

'What is it – Chinese?'

'Thai. They serve English food as well, though. They'd have to, round here – keep the UKIP voters happy.' We'd parked. I unclipped my seatbelt. 'We'd have had the do at the Welfare but it's all boarded up,' I said. 'Has been for years.'

Neither of us made a move to get out. Uncle Peter still had one hand on the wheel.

'I'll be with you in there,' I said. 'You'll be all right.'

Without turning to look at me, he said, 'I only went to crem to pay my respects, Matt. Say goodbye to him. That's all. I weren't planning on any of this.'

'I know. Me neither.'

A few bays along, Suzy, Ben and Laura had climbed out of the VW. My suit jacket was draped over Suzy's arm. She looked hesitant, as if unsure whether to come over.

'Julie and Fiona were dead set against me coming at all,'

Uncle Peter said. *Julie and Fiona.* My cousins. Teenagers, the last time I'd seen them; they would both be pushing fifty, now. 'What you did that night, you and your brother...' He trailed off, shook his head. 'The girls have never forgiven you for that. Sylvia never did, either.'

'That was us, not Dad.'

'He knew you'd done it, though.'

I nodded. 'Yeah.'

'Aye, I thought so.' After a pause, he asked, 'I don't suppose he ever mentioned me – when he were near end?'

I considered lying but just said, 'No. He didn't.' It came out harder than I'd intended.

Suzy was at the passenger door. My uncle pressed the button to lower the window and a gust of heat entered the air-conditioned interior, along with traffic noise and cooking smells.

'Hello,' she said, dipping her head to the window. Smiley, breezy.

I introduced them and she reached awkwardly across me to shake Uncle Peter's hand.

'Do you mind taking Ben and Laura in?' I said. 'We won't be long.'

'Okay.' She didn't look pleased about it.

'Nice lass,' Uncle Peter said, after she'd gone.

'Dad was always asking me if I knew how lucky I was. *Don't blow it*, he used to say. *Tha won't find another one as good, Matt.*' As I spoke his words I heard him saying them. My jaw tightened and it was all I could do not to cry right there in front of my uncle. I took a couple of breaths. 'She doesn't know about that night. Or Ben and Laura.'

'You never told them?' He sounds surprised enough not to believe me.

'I didn't want them to know that about me.'

Uncle Peter sat with his hands in his lap. Smashing his window was such a small matter, set against thirty years of cutting him, and our aunt and cousins, out of our lives.

'Do you ever regret going back?' I asked.

'In Ninety-two?'

'No, Eighty-four.'

He took so long to answer I wondered if he would. Finally, he said, 'There hasn't been a day when I don't. Not one day.'

1984

From her tone of voice, Mam might have been calling with news that someone had died.

'Your uncle has gone back,' she said, just like that.

'Uncle *Peter*?'

'How many other uncles have you got?'

'He can't have.'

'Rich and his mates saw him go past on scab bus not half-hour since.'

I stared at the half-written feature sticking out of my typewriter, as if the meaning of what Mam had said might be encrypted among the words there. 'Are they sure it was him?' With those grilles at the windows, and the speed...I left this thought unspoken. They were sure. You didn't name someone unless you were certain.

'I just phoned Sylvia,' Mam said.

'What did she say?'

'She hung up on me.'

There was a metallic taste in my mouth. 'Have you told Dad?'

'Rich is with him now.'

It was mid-December. The strike had entered its tenth month and, although support was weakening in some areas, around 95 per cent of South Yorkshire was still out. At Withen Main you could count the strike-breakers on one hand. Each day, under police escort, the bus ran the gauntlet, trailing cries of *Scab!*, the meshed glass spattered with phlegm. As I set the phone in its cradle, I pictured Uncle Peter's face at one of those windows – the thick, black brows drawn taut over eyes that stared dead ahead. He wouldn't so much as flick a glance at the pickets jostling with the cordon of police just a few feet from the side of the bus as it sped past. He wouldn't spot my brother, spotting him. But he would know he was there.

My uncle had stood side by side with the men; with Rich, with my dad.

Now he was one of the scabs.

'How can he see his own brother beaten to ground – see him, way he is now?' Mam had said on the phone. 'How can he see *that* and go back to work?'

She blamed Aunt Sylvia. While most of the women in the village had united behind the strike, Sylvia had distanced herself from all of that. At that Sunday dinner, not long after I'd returned from Hong Kong, my aunt had criticised Scargill for not calling a ballot.

'There were a ballot at every pit,' Rich said. 'We voted with us feet.'

'A proper one,' Aunt Sylvia said. 'A national one.'

'And let those cunts in Nottingham vote to shut down our coalfield?'

Mam rapped the table. 'Richard Marron, don't you dare use that word in this house.'

'What, *Nottingham*?' my brother replied. Mam glowered at him, staring him down.

'We'd have got more support from other unions. And from public.' This was Uncle Peter. He shrugged. 'All I'm saying is we gave press and Tories chance to say strike's not valid – to make us out to be nowt but a bunch of yobboes.'

'Arthur knows what he's doing,' Mam said.

'Calling a strike in spring?' Aunt Sylvia asked. 'After NCB had built up coal stocks – after you'd all worked overtime for months to build up stocks for them.'

The argument continued. I took a back seat, not entitled to join in. I'd moved away, I didn't work down the mine. I wasn't going short of food, or struggling to pay bills, or being battered by the police on the picket lines. Away from Withen, though, my semi-detachment made me more radical. At work, whenever I entered the newsroom the other journos would chant *Maggie, Maggie, Maggie – Out, Out, Out!* Aged 23, I was elected Father of Chapel and proposed a motion at the next NUJ branch meeting that we should come out on strike in support of our comrades in the National Union of Mineworkers. The motion was defeated.

Looking back, I can see that I was seeking to assuage my guilt; like a man who has escaped from a sinking ship. That I was seeking, albeit unconsciously, some kind of acceptance – from my brother, from Mam and Dad, from myself – that I was still one of them. That I wasn't too clever for Withen.

By the time I went home for Christmas, Uncle Peter had been back at work two weeks.

'Have you spoken to him?' I asked Dad.

'Why would I d-d-do that?'

'To ask why he's gone back.'

'I know wuh-why – cos they're skint,' he said.

Mam said my uncle's and aunt's electricity and gas had been cut off, and my cousins were going to school in clothes and shoes they'd outgrown, and that the younger one, Fiona, had been diagnosed by the doctor as malnourished. 'Like no other family in Withen is in same boat,' she said. 'Or rest of Yorkshire, or South Wales, or Durham, or Scotland.'

'Puh-puh-Peter's m-made his choice.'

'Or had it made for 'im by Sylvia.'

It was the worst of choices. We aren't a religious family but it carried the weight of a commandment in our house and throughout the mining communities:

Thou shalt not scab.

On Christmas Eve, Rich and I went round to my uncle's house and did what we did.

I'd like to blame it on the beer, but we weren't too drunk to know what we were up to.

I'd like to say I tried to dissuade my brother. But I didn't.

Once the village got wind of what we'd done to one of our own, it was open season on Uncle Peter. In the following weeks, other windows were smashed, dog shit was pushed through the letter-box, the shed in the back yard was set alight, SCAB and SCUM were daubed on the front door and on the chipboard panels he'd fixed over the windows. If they ventured into the village, my uncle, aunt and cousins were sworn at, spat at. Julie and Fiona were frozen out at school; friendless. In the shops, no-one would serve Aunt Sylvia. One evening, when he went to the end of the street to post a letter, Uncle Peter was set upon by three men and beaten so badly he spent nearly as long in hospital as Dad had done.

I can't say whether my brother was responsible for some or any of these incidents. He insisted, has always insisted, that he wasn't.

'I said all I had to say when I stood in his garden after we'd done his windows.'

From that night on, they were dead to us.

2014

In the lobby of the Emerald Buddha sat a wooden Buddha, painted green – a serene, slimline Siddhartha Gautama, not the fat, jolly version. He was in the lotus position, hands configured in a symbolic gesture that I might once have been able to interpret. I ushered my uncle into the bar area, expecting a scene from a western, where a crowded saloon falls silent. But there were a few turned heads, that was all. I couldn't immediately spot my brother.

'Beer?' I asked Uncle Peter.

'Not when I'm driving.'

'It spills going round bends,' I said, supplying the punchline to one of his gags.

'You remember my jokes, then?'

'They're all in the British Museum, now.'

He gave a wheezy laugh. We were passing through the throng, Uncle Peter struggling due to his hip. I muttered *excuse me* and *thanks* as people made way for us.

'I'll come to bar with you,' he said, sticking close to me.

'It's all right.' I pointed. 'Suzy and our two are over there.'

As I steered him in their direction, we came upon Mam, sitting with a neighbour from the sheltered housing. They had glasses of sherry in front of them. We both paused, as if it had been our purpose all along to approach her table. Her semi-vacant gaze settled on each of us in turn and I heard her murmur to the woman beside her, 'Who's that chap with my Don?'

'It's me, Mam. Matt.'

She smiled at me as if I'd said something silly.

'Mam, this is Uncle Peter.'

'What did he say?' she asked her companion.

'Uncle Peter,' I repeated. 'He came to pay his respects to Dad.'

'You had a brother called Peter,' she said, addressing my uncle. Then, to her friend, 'I were a bridesmaid at their wedding. Don were best man.' She looked up at Uncle Peter. 'What were her name, love – Peter's wife?'

'Sylvia,' Uncle Peter said, quietly.

Mam frowned. Took a sip of sherry. 'No, that weren't it.'

She lost interest in us. We stood there pointlessly for a moment before moving on.

'Poor bloody woman,' my uncle said. 'When you think how she used to be.'

On my way to order drinks, I passed a seating plan at the entrance to the dining area: twenty tables, four on each. Me,

Suzy, Ben and Laura had been put together at one of the top tables.

'We'll be calling everyone through in a few minutes, sir.'

It was the *maitre d'*. Indicating our table on the plan, I said, 'Sorry to be a nuisance, but could you lay an extra place at No. 2, please?'

I was at the bar when Rich drew up beside me. He gazed straight ahead at the spirit optics. 'What you doing, Matt?' Casual. He might've been asking me to recommend a whisky.

'Buying our uncle an orange juice.'

My brother gave me a sidelong look.

'It's been thirty years,' I said.

'Once a scab—'

'Christ, Rich, spare me the fucking clichés.'

'Cliché. Right.' He placed his hands on the edge of the counter, as if about to perform a set of bench-presses. 'You going to *announce* him? Make another of your speeches?'

I let that go. 'We don't have the right to turn a man away from his brother's funeral.'

'There. Jot it down on one of them fucking cards of yours so you don't forget it.'

The barmaid set an orange juice and a pint in front of me. If she'd heard what we'd said, you wouldn't have known. She'd smiled, before, when I greeted her with *sawat dee* – but politely, as if humouring me. I was glad Rich hadn't been there to witness that.

'Or are you going to flog a piece to *Guardian*?' my brother asked, when she'd moved away to serve someone else. '*The uncle who came in from the cold*.'

'D'you remember him making a set of battery operated floodlights for your Subbuteo pitch?' I said. 'Or when he used to take us tobogganing at Rother Valley? Or him stopping Dad from giving you a belting that time you—'

'I remember him crossing picket line,' Rich cut in. 'Going

back to work when Dad were still having blackouts from where that bastard copper had knacked him.'

'You can't blame Uncle Peter for what happened to Dad.'

'We lost strike cos of cunts like him.'

I shook my head. 'The strike was already lost by the time he went back.'

'Oh aye? Were that the word on street, then, Matt, down in fucking London?'

Our raised voices had drawn the attention of some of those standing nearby. We fell quiet for a moment. I sipped my pint. The beer was sharp and hoppy.

We *had* blamed our uncle. Me included. After he'd turned scab, we came to hold him responsible for the way Dad was after Orgreave. Uncle Peter left Withen Main – left mining – in May '85, two months after the end of the strike. The men wouldn't work with him. He left the village, then, as well – him, Aunt Sylvia, the two girls. They didn't tell anyone, they just went. Dad, meanwhile, stayed on at the colliery until it closed. But he wasn't able to do the same work as before; they took him off the face and put him above ground, on to the screens, sifting waste material from the coal that other men had mined. It was a job usually allocated to lads or old-timers, or miners with disabilities. If he'd lost confidence after his head injury, the switch to unskilled work brought him lower still.

None of it was Uncle Peter's fault. But we made a correlation between our father's decline and our uncle's absence. His betrayal. Dad never admitted as much but, with the loss of his brother, he'd lost another vital piece of himself.

'What d'you think Dad would've made of this place?' I asked.

Rich frowned, as if taking a moment to adjust to the change of subject. 'They used to come here for Sunday lunch, sometimes – him and Mam.'

'Seriously?' I took in the black-and-gold decor, the diffused lighting, the low-slung, furniture, the wall-prints of seated, standing and reclining Buddhas. Bangkok meets IKEA.

'They do a proper carvery,' Rich said. 'Special rate for OAPs.'

'Dad was always one for a carvery. *Pile it high and shovel it down.*'

Rich didn't have anything to say to that. We lapsed into another, briefer silence.

'I'm going to take his drink over,' I said, finally.

'Leave it where it is,' my brother said, 'and take him back to his car.'

'No, Rich. I'm not doing that.'

We were eight and ten, kicking a ball in the back lane; twelve and fourteen, in the school playground. We were 21 and 23, in Uncle Peter's garden on Christmas Eve, 1984.

Rich stared at the glass of orange juice, as if debating whether to send it crashing to the floor. But his hands remained braced against the bar. His shoulders relaxed.

Looking me square in the face, he said, 'Dad wouldn't have wanted him here.'

'Probably not, no.'

Rich nodded. 'You always were a selfish fucker, Matt.'

In the corner, Suzy had managed to snaffle a seat for Uncle Peter. He sat with one leg bent, the other straight out in front of him. She was squatting beside his chair, showing him the photos she kept in her purse of Ben and Laura when they were little.

I handed my uncle his drink.

'All right?' Suzy asked. She must have seen me talking to Rich.

'Yeah,' I said. 'Everything's sorted.'

18th June 1984

I can only piece this together from the fragments I've been told and from my imagination:

They leave Withen after first light in Uncle Peter's brown Allegro (the one with the boot that won't shut when it's open and won't open when it's shut.) My uncle drives, Dad sits in the front passenger seat, my brother is in the back. Rich has joined the picket at the coking plant several times in the preceding weeks but this is the first time for Dad and Uncle Peter. They're in a convoy streaming out of the village. A glorious day is forecast but the sun has yet to dissolve the slicks of mist in the fields. The men's breaths steam up the windows and my uncle steers one-handed as he wipes the windscreen with a grubby yellow chammy. Dad will be craving a cigarette but smoking isn't allowed in the car, by order of Aunt Sylvia. Rich rubs his palms on his thighs, the way he does when he's nervous. Dad hums under his breath: Tom Jones, 'The Green, Green Grass of Home'. He doesn't even realise he's doing it.

Half a world away, in Kowloon, it's lunchtime; Becca and I are grabbing a bite to eat between tutorials. I doubt I'll be giving my dad, my brother, my uncle, a moment's thought.

'Let's have some music,' Uncle Peter says, turning on the radio.

Over whichever song is playing, he asks if they've brought packed lunches – *snap*, he calls it – and Dad snorts and says, 'What is this, Pete – a fucking school trip?'

They all laugh.

'Hey, Richard.' My uncle glances in the rearview mirror. 'Nice perm by the way.'

'It's not a perm,' my brother says.

'I thought it were Kevin Keegan in back for a minute there.'

'It's *not* a fucking perm.'

'Looks like one from where I'm sat.'

Rich doesn't say anything. Just scowls out of the car window.

'Well I reckon it suits him,' Dad says. 'All he needs is a spandex suit and he could enter Eurovision.'

'It's not a *perm*, all right,' Rich says, 'it's a fucking *demi-wave*.'

There's a brief pause, then all three of them are laughing like it's the funniest thing they've ever heard.

They're still laughing when the news comes on. Uncle Peter shushes the other two. The newsreader refers to the strike, *entering its 16th week*. Perhaps in relation to this item, or a different one, the prime minister's husky, carefully modulated tones issue from the speaker. Rich leans forward between the front seats, intending to turn off the radio. But my uncle has beaten him to it.

Thatcher falls abruptly silent.

'That fucking woman.' This will be Dad. He can't hear her voice, or see her face, without calling her *that fucking woman*. Or *that woman*, if Mam's around.

I picture him, glaring at the dial, as if the radio is responsible for Thatcher; or as if Thatcher herself is hidden behind the black, plastic fascia and might start speaking again.

'Even wi' radio off, I can still hear that voice,' Rich says.

'She could be dead in her grave,' Uncle Peter says, 'and we'd still not shut her up.'

The convoy crests a hill, opening up a sweeping view towards Sheffield: the motorway, the twin cooling towers at Tinsley. And, there, the coking plant – glinting beneath the risen sun like a space station from the cover of a sci-fi magazine.

'Here we go, boys,' my uncle says.

Rich takes it up, quietly at first. 'Here we go, here we go, here we go...'

Uncle Peter joins in, '... here we go, here we go, here we go-o...'

Then Dad, '... here we go, here we go, here we go, here we go-o-o, *here we go.*'

Rich is beating out the rhythm on his knee, Dad is rapping the dashboard, Uncle Peter thumping the steering wheel with the heel of his hand, three voices united as one: 'HERE WE GO, HERE WE GO, HERE WE GO, HERE WE GO, HERE WE GO, HERE WE GO-O; HERE WE GO, HERE WE GO, HERE WE GO, HERE WE GO-O-O, *HERE WE GO!*'

2014

The *maitre d'* banged a small gong and invited us all to take our seats for lunch. Our corner of the bar was farthest away, so most of the other mourners had already gone through by the time the five of us filed into to the restaurant.

The top tables stood beneath the far windows. Sunshine streamed in, brilliant against the white walls and tablecloths. The Withen Main Lodge banner hung from a wall – huge, dominant – its reds, yellows and purples shimmering, the portrayed figures so etched with brightness they were translucent, ghostlike. The last time I'd seen it was on 3rd March 1985, swaying on poles at the head of the procession through the village, as the men – my father and brother among them – returned to work at the end of the strike. They marched behind Withen's colliery band, heads held so high you would think they had won.

'We *have* wuh-wuh-won,' Dad said, that day. 'You only l-lose if you don't fight.'

As we approached the top tables, I was peripherally aware of Mam, and Rich, Tanya and their kids, already in their seats. Watching us. I led the way, then Uncle Peter, with Suzy at his side, helping him, followed by Ben and Laura.

So I was the first to see what had been done.

The table was stripped.

No chairs arranged around it, no tablecloth draped over it. No place mats, no plates, no knives and forks, no spoons, no wine glasses, no water glasses, no napkins, no jug of water, no basket of bread rolls, no butter dish, no salt, no pepper, no small vase of flowers. No name cards. Just a number 2 clipped to a stand in the centre of the bare wooden table.

About the Author

Martyn Bedford is the author of five novels for adults: *Acts of Revision*, which won the Yorkshire Post Best First Work Award, *Exit, Orange & Red*, *The Houdini Girl*, *Black Cat*, and *The Island of Lost Souls*. He is also the author of three novels for young adults: *Flip* (shortlisted for the Costa Children's Book Award, and winner of four awards including the Sheffield Children's Book Award and Calderdale Book of the Year), *Never Ending*, and *Twenty Questions for Gloria*, winner of the 2017 Coventry Inspiration Book Award. Between them, his novels have been translated into fifteen languages.

Martyn has contributed to five Comma anthologies: The *Book of Leeds*, *M.O.*, *Beta-Life*, *Spindles*, and *Protest*. He is a senior lecturer in creative writing at Leeds Trinity University.